DANGEROUS AFFAIR

DANGEROUS AFFAIR

S. E. ISAAC

J. TRUESDELL

Dangerous Affair

Copyright © 2023 **J. Truesdell, S.E. Isaac**

CHAPTER ONE
EVA

I stood in front of the full-length mirror, staring at my reflection. I was dreading this evening. I had ever since I learned I would be attending. I hate the thought of standing in a small room, watching a bunch of men playing a card game, poker to be exact, hoping to win millions. Smoking, and drinking, while I stood there looking pretty and pretending to care. Many of them were already multi-million-aires, yet there was something about this game that tempted them. Maybe it was the excitement of the game? Maybe it was the fear of losing when none of them have ever experienced it. Either way, I hated it.

I had only been to one before, when Carter, my boyfriend, had pleaded with me to go back when we had first started dating. I had stood near the back of the room, watching the men try to outdo one another.

Carter hadn't played, but I could see in his eyes how entranced he was with it, how desperately he wanted to be a part of it. He had told me later that evening that the game was exclusive, only a rare few were ever invited to join. If one was invited, it was considered a privilege and honor to be included. To even be invited, if only to watch, was also considered an honor. It meant that you were someone of importance. It was also an opportunity to make connections.

Since then, we haven't been back. That had been six years ago. I had hoped Carter had forgotten about those games, but I quickly learned that wasn't the case. He came to me a week ago, telling me he had finally been invited to join the game, not just watch, but to actually play this time. He had been excited and confident that he was now considered one of the elite. He explained that this game was the biggest one of the year. All the top players would be in attendance. Without thought, I was stupid and voiced that I didn't want to attend. The thought of standing there for hours was not appealing to me at all. It was a mistake that had cost me dearly.

Carter had grown furious with me, telling me it was my duty to be there, to be by his side and support him. Things had gotten worse from that moment on. He began accusing me of seeing someone behind his back, asking me if that was my reasoning for not wanting to go, that I was planning on secretly meeting someone. It had spiraled downward from there. Thinking back on it now, I realize I should have known better.

I knew never to push him and I should never, ever anger him. It would never end well for me, and I had the scars and bruises to prove it.

Carter had changed so much over the years we have been together. Growing angrier each day and more violent. It wasn't always physical either. Carter was the type that used his words as well. To tear me down. Belittle me. Make me feel like I was unworthy. Why did I stay? I would ask myself that question every single day, never coming up with an answer. Perhaps I stay out of fear. I knew if I ever left, nothing would stop Carter from bringing me back. Or perhaps it was because I had nowhere else to go. I had no family, no one I could turn to. It was just me. Had been that way since I was sixteen.

I inhale a deep breath to calm my nerves as I check my makeup one last time. Everything needed to be perfect for Carter, even the way I was dressed. He desperately wants to impress these men at the game. I raise my eyes to my own in my reflection and was shocked to see the lack of emotion within their depths. My eyes seem cold and empty. I gave a small, humorless chuckle and turned from the mirror. Cold and empty. That is exactly how I have been feeling for a long while now.

I move to my dresser and open my jewelry box, pulling out the necklace and earring set Carter wants me to wear. It was his mother's jewelry and worth a great deal of money. I knew his reasoning for wanting me to wear them. It was to impress, to allow the others in that room to think he was as wealthy as they were.

The truth was, Carter was not as rich. All the money he had was given to him by his father. But when his father saw how Carter was squandering it away, he had quickly cut him off. Now Carter was looking to gain all that had been taken, to try and prove to his father that he can handle it. But the reality was, he couldn't. I knew what would happen if he manages to win tonight. In a month, he would be back right where he was.

I place the earrings in my ears and was about to put on the necklace when the door to the room opened and Carter stepped inside. He paused just inside the door and let his eyes travel up and down the length of my body, appraising how I look. He smiles and then closes the door behind him before making his way over to where I stood.

Carter reaches out and takes the necklace from my hands, then motions for me to turn around. He moves my long brunette hair to the side and places the necklace around my neck. I tip my head slightly as he did the clasp, then I felt his hot breath against my skin.

"You will behave yourself tonight, Eva. You will be attentive and supportive. Understood?" He asks, the threat clear in his tone.

I felt a chill run down my spine at his calm words.

"I would never do anything to embarrass you," I reassure him.

"That's a good girl." Then he leans in and places a kiss on my neck before moving away.

I took another deep breath to steady myself, then turn, plastering on a smile as I watch Carter reach for my wrap. He motions for me to come closer, then drapes the silk over my shoulders.

"Are you ready?" He asks as his fingers brush along my cheek. I smile and nod my head, slipping my hand into the crook of his arm when he offers it to me. I hold my head high as he leads me from the room, down the grand staircase to the waiting limousine that Carter had acquired for the night. I didn't ask him how he had been able to. To do so would have caused him to be angry and tonight of all nights, I need to keep him as calm as possible.

The driver of the limo was waiting for us and quickly opens the door. I wanted to smile at the man, but knew better. If Carter saw, he would accuse me of liking the man and wanting to bed him. Instead, I lower my eyes, refusing to make eye contact with him.

I slip inside the car and move to the far left of the seat, waiting for Carter to join me. He pauses and speaks to the driver for a moment, then slips inside, taking the seat beside me. Moments later, I feel the car pull away from the house and down the long driveway.

Carter grins at me, then places his hand between my thighs. "You look beautiful tonight," He says as his hand rises higher and higher up my leg. I want to place my hand over his, to stop him from going higher, but I remain still as his fingers brush along the silk of my panties.

"I'd take you right now, but I'd hate to ruin your dress." He rubs my sex over my panties roughly with his thumb, causing me to inhale sharply, but not out of want.

"After I win tonight. I'll tear the dress from you and fuck you in front of everyone." With any other person, I would take those words as bold talk. But I knew Carter well enough to know that he would do just that if it meant he would look like a god in front of those he wishes to impress.

He watches me as he slips his finger beneath the edge of my panties, then between my folds before pushing the single digit inside of me, causing me to gasp slightly. He watches my eyes as he pumps his finger in and out before pulling it away and lifting it to his lips. I smile at him, letting him believe I enjoyed that and wanted more. I was getting quite good at faking my emotions where he was concerned.

"Fuck, you taste so good," he says as he licks his lips and then turns to the front, looking out the windshield. Of course, he never raised the divider glass, so their chauffeur had seen and heard everything. Which was probably what Carter wanted. Quickly, I turn away, looking out the side window. I fear if I hadn't, he would see the disgust in my eyes. Not once had I spoken. I rarely did around Carter. He was the type that believed women should be seen and not heard, much like children.

"Maybe you could suck me off before we get there," Carter adds, his hand back on my thigh.

I swallowed back the bile at the very thought and turn to him with a smile.

"It would ruin my makeup, and I want to look my best for you tonight," I say sweetly, hoping he would let it go and not force me to do as he asks. Carter glances at the driver, who I notice was looking back at us through the rearview mirror.

"Later then, when we celebrate." He replies as he shifts in his seat. I fear I angered him by not agreeing, but to do as he asks now, I would surely vomit. Thankfully, Carter fell silent from that moment on, watching as we travel down the road toward the city limits.

It only took a short time before we reached the town and made our way through the busy streets. I watch the people as they walk the sidewalks, staring into the windows of shops, or seated at a restaurant's table enjoying a nice dinner. Many were laughing and having a good time. I felt an ache building within my chest. Seeing others happy often did that to me.

We turn onto the expressway and make our way toward the more posh part of town. Ten minutes later, we arrived at our destination. The limo pulled up in front of a large mansion and comes to a halt.

A minute later, the door opens and Carter climbs out. I wait for him to offer me his hand, but he sees someone of importance and moves away. With a sigh, I slip from the car, noticing the frown on the chauffeur's face at my escort's rudeness. He inclines his head to me, in greeting, then closes the door to the limo once I'm clear.

Like a good girl that I pretend to be, I quickly move closer to where Carter stands.

He is talking and boasting about anything and everything that makes him look like he was someone special. I slip my hand into his arm and wait for him to finish before leading me inside.

The house was exquisite. The furnishing is pristine, the crystal chandelier that hangs from the ceiling twinkles in the light. I watch as couples greet one another while the servants walk around with champagne flutes on trays. I had always thought this was the type of life I wanted, but the years have slowly changed that.

Carter accepts a glass from the server, but I politely decline. Carter insists I not drink tonight. He said it makes women weaker and numb to their surroundings. He wants me to stay alert and attentive.

I glance around the room, looking at everyone that has gathered. I knew most, but many I had never met. There was a man I have never seen before, standing near the back of the room. I watch as he scans the room, looking at all in attendance. Something about him oozes power. His hair was cut short, his jaw clean-shaven. He was tall, well over six feet, and even through his suit jacket, I knew he was muscular. His eyes land on mine and the corner of his mouth curls up in a devilish grin, sending a shiver racing throughout my body. He inclines his head and raises his glass to me. Quickly, I turn away.

"Remember what I said." Carter leans over and whispers.

I nearly jump, having been so enthralled with the man across the room, that I nearly forgot my place.

I turn my head and smile at Carter, as sweetly as I could, and whisper the words, "Of course, my love." The last words nearly choking me, but it soothes Carter when I speak them. Carter smiles, then turns to the room.

"See that man standing near the back?" He motions to the man I had been watching just moments earlier.

I felt a twinge of panic in the pit of my stomach. Had Carter seen me looking at him? My heart raced. Was he about to accuse me of flirting with him?

"The one in the black suit?" I ask, my voice soft when I speak. I pretend not to know which one he was talking about. Maybe Carter hadn't seen anything.

"Yes, that's him. His name is Marco Giodano. One of the richest men here tonight. He is the one I need to beat." As if saying his name aloud calls to him, the man lifts his eyes to mine once again. I felt a tingle of excitement rush through me when our eyes meet. "Once I've beaten him, they'll all know I am a force to reckon with."

I stare across the room at the man. Somehow I had a feeling that will be easier said than done. He didn't look like the type of man that could be easily beaten.

CHAPTER TWO
MARCO

Fuck, she's perfect, I thought, taking in the sight of the woman.

She's gorgeous from head to toe. Her long brown hair standing out against her red dress is what caught my eye. The way her dress clung to her in all the right places is what made my eyes continue to roam across her body. She stands out in the crowd, making the rest of the women in the room disappear.

She is nothing like the other women who are here tonight to attend my monthly poker night party. The women scattered throughout the room, clinging to an arm of a man, are all wearing low-cut, short dresses. The kind you would expect a stripper to wear. They are here with one goal in mind–to win a man over–to either get into his bed or into his bank account.

Either way, there is nothing special about them and they annoy me with their fakeness. The woman standing next to Carter Montgomery is different. I can tell by her eyes that she has zero interest in being here, and that excites me.

"Giovanni," I whisper to my underboss, who is standing to my right.

"Yes, Boss?" he asks with his eyes on me.

"Who is she?"

He follows my eyes to the woman, chuckles, then looks back at me.

"That's Eva Merrick. She's Carter Montgomery's girl," he replies.

The one person who wasn't supposed to get an invite had brought the best guest to my party. I guess I should thank Giovanni for persuading me to send an invitation to the dickhead. I still wasn't sure why he wanted Carter to be here, but I always trusted his judgment, even if Carter's smug face made me want to bash his face in.

Carter Montgomery wasn't like the rest of us in this room. His money came from his daddy's handouts and then he pissed it all away on drugs, luxury items, and women. None of whom were the ones standing next to him.

How could he fucking cheat on a woman like her? I mutter to myself.

"If looks could kill, he'd fall over dead, Boss," Giovanni chuckles faintly beside me.

I glance at Giovanni and shrug. He nods, then goes back to sipping his drink.

"If he makes a scene tonight, you *will* take care of it," I remind him.

"If he forgets his place, I'll end him without hesitation, Boss," he replies with a nod.

"Good," I say, setting my glass of whiskey down and clapping my hands together.

Conversations and laughter continue as though I didn't exist, except for my guys, who are scattered throughout the room. I glance at Giovanni and then Ivan, one of my enforcers. They both stare at the crowd in disgust.

"When the Boss speaks, you all shut the fuck up!" Ivan roars. His words echo throughout the room. The whole room falls silent. All eyes are on him but quickly fall onto me.

I can't help but smirk because this is the way I like things. When I am unsatisfied, one of my guys takes care of the problem. No matter how big or how small. The problem is always resolved swiftly or heads roll.

"I'm so glad to have all of your attention. Gentleman…" I look around the room and bring my gaze back to the woman next to Carter. When our eyes meet, I smile, "Ladies."

She quickly lowers her gaze; however, I can still see her blushing. Carter glances at her. His jaw clenches, he balls his fist, and he looks at me with rage-filled eyes. His annoyance only adds to my need for the woman next to him.

At this rate, by the end of the night, Eva Merrick was going to be mine.

"For those who don't know me, I am Marco Giodano," my words are directed at Eva and her alone.

Her cheeks redden and she lowers her head. I grin and turn my attention from her. "Most of you have been here a time or two."

Several of the men chuckle and nod their heads.

"The rules in my home haven't changed. If you don't like them, you can leave now," I continue with my speech, looking over the room. "If you stay and violate *any* of them, I can assure you that you *will* be punished. No questions asked. No excuses accepted."

My eyes land back on Eva, who is staring at me with wide eyes. She looks absolutely terrified. I watch as she swallows long and hard. She's clearly new to my world or else she would know that I never hurt women. No matter what they do.

"Women," I say, looking Eva in her eyes and hoping like hell she'll believe me, "are an exception. Always."

She seems to calm slightly, but the fear is still there. Fear is the last thing I want to strike into her. Once things settle, I'll steal her away from Carter and explain things. Regardless if Carter likes it or not.

"Giovanni will explain the rest. Play fair and let's have a good night," I finish my half-ass speech. Who the fuck can concentrate around Eva? She's mind consuming and she doesn't even try to be.

The room fills with polite applause. No doubt because they fear my wrath. I suppose fake claps are better than none.

"I'll be in the room," I mutter, walking past the guys toward the V.I.P. room.

Ivan and two of my other enforcers–Lorenzo and Dario–follow closely as I make my way through the crowded room. Everyone quickly moves out of the way. In no time, I'm taking my seat at the head of the main poker table.

"Hey, Boss," Clarice, who is dealing tonight at my table, smiles brightly.

"Clarice," I acknowledge. She blushes slightly and twirls a strand of her red hair that is dangling down.

Her dealer outfit is snug, pushing her breasts damn near out the top of her white button-up shirt. Her black mini skirt accentuated her long, slender legs and round ass. She's every guy's fantasy.

"I'm sure you're going to win all of it, Boss. You're the best card player in New York," she boasts. "Maybe even the best player in the entire country. No one can beat you, Boss. *No. One.*"

On a normal night, her flirtiness would be a turn on. I might even go as far as to have her get me off before the games started. Not tonight. Tonight, there's only one woman on my mind.

Fuck, I growl, realizing that I don't even know Eva and already she's fucking with my head.

CHAPTER THREE
EVA

I watch as Marco leaves the room, making his way into what I assume to be the room the game will be held in. I lick my lips, remembering how he controlled the room. How he commanded attention from everyone there. Carter clung to every one of his words, the women… all held the same look in their eyes as he spoke. It was obvious what they wanted. To share his bed. I'd be a fool to admit that he did not get my heart racing, especially as he held my eyes while he spoke. He was sexy and oozed danger. The type of man every mother tells her daughter to stay away from, yet the very type of man a woman couldn't help but be drawn to.

Carter places his hand on my upper arm, startling me, and squeezes tightly. Without a word, he guides me away from the crowd, to a more private place. Once we were there, he leans in and harshly whispers in my ear.

"What the fuck was that? He couldn't keep his eyes off you." I felt my entire body stiffen as the grip on my arm tightened.

"Carter… ,"

"You want to fuck him, don't you? He's been eye fucking you all night." He growls as he turns me so that I am facing him.

"What? No. I don't…" I say, panic rising inside me. What I had feared earlier was now happening. Because I glanced at another, Carter was now furious. His insecurities rushing to the surface.

"Bullshit. I saw the way you were looking at him." He hisses. "You want him between your legs. His dick inside you." He snarls.

"I wasn't… Carter, I don't want anyone but you," I lie, hoping to calm the situation. He squeezes my arm tighter, and I wince. "You're hurting me," I say, my voice rising slightly.

One of the guards appears. He looks at Carter, then at me. "Is everything alright?" he asks, as he looks back at Carter.

Carter releases me, then smiles. "Yes, everything is fine." He wraps his arm around my shoulder and pulls me closer to his body. "Isn't that right, Sweetheart?" He says sweetly as if there was nothing wrong. The anger that had been in his voice, was gone. For now.

Both men look at me, waiting for my answer. I glance up at Carter, knowing that if I say anything that would oppose what he was saying, things would be much worse for me. So I did what I had to do.

"Everything is fine." I smile at the guard.

The man stares at me, watching me. After a minute, he inclines his head. "Proceed to the game room, please." He says before he turns and walks away.

Carter glances around, noticing a few people looking in our direction. By the look on their faces, it was obvious they had heard something. They turn from us and began heading into the room, just as it is announced the game would be starting soon.

Carter removes his arm from my shoulder and looks at me. Anger back in his eyes. He turns, watching everyone move away from us. I knew when we return home later, it would get bad. I had done nothing wrong, yet Carter believes otherwise. I knew I would be punished severely for this. Suddenly, the look on his face changes, going from anger to something else. He smiles at me.

"This could be to my benefit."

An icy feeling of dread washes over me at that moment. I want to ask him what he meant but before I could; he grips my hand and leads me towards the room. We enter and he pauses.

"Clearly, our host is smitten with you, so I want you to use that. Gain his attention and distract him from the game." He leans in and brushes his lips over mine, then whispers.

"Be the slut I know you are." He held my eyes before kissing me again, then starts to lead me towards a table.

I walk silently, fighting back fear as I glance around the room. I had done everything he wanted me to do.

I played the perfect, doting girlfriend, hoping to avoid any issues. Yet because I did nothing more than look at someone, Carter was furious. This was everything I had hoped to avoid. It was why I wanted no part of this game. His request of me caused even more panic to fill me. If I do as he asks, he may punish me for it later, saying I enjoyed it. I was in a damned if I do and damned if I don't situation and had no idea how to get myself out of it.

Carter pulls out one of the chairs at the table where our host was seated, but before he could sit, a man appears.

"Sir, not here. Your table is in the back." The man says, motioning to the back of the room.

Carter looks at him, then at the table, the man points out, a frown appearing on his face. "Back there? I thought I would be seated here, at the main table?" he argues.

"All games have been selected. Your name was picked to be seated there. If you win your game, you will be placed at another table. So on and so on until only five players remain. You were told this when you received your invitation." The guard motions to the table. "Take your seat, sir. The games are about to begin. If you have not placed your bet before it starts, you will be immediately disqualified and escorted from the premises."

Carter looks at the man, then at our host. Knowing he had no other choice but to comply. I could feel his eyes on me - Marco's eyes. I glance up and find him watching me. I felt my heart race at the way he was looking at me.

The intensity of his gaze. Marco grins, then turns his attention to Carter, clearly amused by what was happening between Carter and the man.

Carter, having no other choice, turns away and heads to the back of the room. I silently follow, but not before I look at Marco, discovering his attention back on me. He lifts his glass and nods in my direction. He takes a sip of his drink, but not once does he take his eyes off me. I feel my pulse quicken. This man was causing me problems tonight yet, I found myself excited by it. I turn away and follow Carter to the back, trying my best not to smile.

We reach his table and Carter finds his seat, just as the poker chips were being handed out. I knew those boxes that were being placed next to each player were worth millions of dollars. A woman approaches Carter, asking how much he wants. He spoke softly, then hands over his money to claim his box. When a server approaches him he ordered a drink, not bothering to see if I wanted anything. Carter's focus was now fully on the game.

I knew he was determined to win. His goal was to end up at the main table and become the last man to hold it all. Anything less and he would feel as though he failed. A box was placed down next to him and once everyone had their chips, the dealer took her seat. She spoke a few words, then dealt out the cards. The games had begun.

Cater glances over at me as I take my place near the wall, close to his table. He watches me for a moment, then turns his attention to the game.

I take that moment to look over where our host was seated. He was looking down at his cards, then, as if sensing me watching, he lifted his eyes to mine, the corner of his mouth curving into a heart-stopping grin.

CHAPTER FOUR
MARCO

The spark in Eva's eyes has dwindled. She looks almost lifeless. What the fuck had Carter said to her? I saw him pull her off to the side, but they fell out of view. Erik, another one of my enforcers, was the one who went around the corner to where they were and spoke to them.

"Ivan?" I call out. He's standing a few feet behind me and quickly walks over to my side.

"Yes, Boss?" he asks.

"Bring me Erik," I command.

"You got it, Boss," he replies, disappearing to go find Erik.

"Everything good, Boss?" Giovanni whispers to my right. I glance at him, nod, and then look back at Eva.

She's no longer looking in my direction. Her eyes are lowered to the ground.

She's biting her bottom lip nervously and tapping her foot against the floor. She looks scared to death.

"Ah. Carter must have said something to her," Giovanni says.

"He better pray that's not the case," I growl under my breath, returning my attention back to my cards.

The thought of Eva unhappy pisses me off. I don't know much about her; however, that doesn't stop me from wanting to protect her. I want to protect her from Carter and every other asshole in this world.

"Your call, Mr. Giodano," Clarice says sweetly. I look up from my cards and find everyone around the table staring at me anxiously.

"I'll raise 2k," I reply, picking up two blue chips. I flip them into the pile of chips already in the center of the table. Several people's eyes widen as though two thousand dollars is too much for me to afford. "Is there a problem? Too low?"

My eyes narrow as my temper flares. Before any of them can respond, I toss a gold chip worth ten grand into the pile of chips. Giovanni chuckles and leans back in his seat.

"Anyone else want to raise?" Clarice smiles, looking around at the others.

They all reply with a groan and then toss their cards down. I flip my cards over, revealing my shit hand. Every mother fucker sitting there is pissed off at themselves for not calling my bluff.

"Winner is Mister Giodano," Clarice says cheerfully, sweeping the chips over to me. Giovanni stands and stacks them, as Clarice gathers the cards.

"This shit isn't even fun," I mutter softly to Giovanni.

"Want me to get new players over here?" he whispers, still stacking the chips. I shake my head.

"No," I look over at Eva. She lifts her gaze to mine and quickly lowers it. "Where the fuck is Erik?"

As though he heard me, he and Ivan round the corner and head over to my table.

"You wanted to see me, Boss?" Erik asks in a soft tone.

"What the fuck did Carter say to Eva?" I ask, looking up at him. He seems confused by the names, so I point at Eva. He looks where I'm pointing, then turns to where his back is facing her. He leans down to my ear.

"The guy was giving her a firm talking to. He was pretty pissed. Accused her of basically being a whore. Told her to use her charm to distract you so he could win," he whispers. "He had a pretty hard hold on her. That's why I stepped in; otherwise, I would have just kept eavesdropping, Boss." He stands tall and waits for me to speak.

My blood is fucking boiling. Carter was rough handling Eva? And in my fucking home? Unacceptable.

"Oh, shit," Giovanni says. "Boss, you good?"

"Stop the fucking game," I snap.

My table and all the players at the table to my right are staring at me. Probably because I'm not even trying to whisper. I give zero fucks at this point.

Carter is going to answer for this.

"Bring two chairs over here and put them right here," I point to my left. "Then someone go grab that dickhead and Eva. I don't care if you have to drag him by his fucking neck."

"You've got it, Boss," Ivan and Erik reply in unison. They hurry off and retrieve two chairs, then bring them back over to where I asked them to put them.

"Ask Eva if she'd join me over here and tell dickhead to get the fuck over here *now*," I order.

"Our pleasure, Boss," Ivan grins, then he and Erik walk over to Carter's table.

Erik approaches Eva and talks to her, while Ivan deals with Carter. Eva looks over at me. I smile and gesture at one of the empty seats. She looks nervously at Carter, who is glaring at her. I start to stand, but Giovanni puts his hand on my shoulder.

"Let me take care of your light work, Boss. I'm the one who invited him after all," he chuckles, but not his normal chuckle. This is one coated with venom. He's ready to go to work on Carter.

"Two minutes."

"Won't take me more than twenty seconds." He doesn't say another word, just stands up and storms over to Carter's table. He points at Eva and then back towards me without looking.

Eva nervously stands up. She teeters on her feet and Erik offers her an arm. Normally, I'd be pissed off, but I can tell she really needs the support. Eva politely declines.

Carter stands up and faces Erik.

Clearly ready to butt heads with him. Giovanni leans over and whispers something in Carter's ear. Carter's body tenses before he turns and looks at me.

I can't help the scowl that's etched on my face. Right now, there's no one I hate more in this world than Carter Montgomery. Before tonight, I couldn't stand him and now, after knowing how he treats Eva, I despise him even more.

Carter stares long and hard at me. He glances at Eva and then back at me. A smug grin crosses his face.

This mother fucker, I say to myself.

"Boss? You want me to–" Eddie asks behind me out of nowhere. I had forgotten he was even standing back there.

"Giovanni will take care of it or I will personally," I reply with my eyes still locked on Carter.

"Understood, Boss."

I watch as Eva timidly follows behind Giovanni and Carter. Erik is a few steps behind her, carrying Carter's chips. They soon arrive at the table. I gesture to the two empty chairs and Carter begins to sit down in the chair closest to me.

"No," I shake my head. "Miss Merrick will sit there."

Carter opens his mouth to protest several times but eventually makes the decision to keep his mouth shut.

Guess you aren't as stupid as I thought, I muse to myself.

"Miss Merrick, do me the honors and sit beside me," I say, standing up and pulling the chair out from the table. The entire room falls silent.

Eva's cheeks redden. She looks cautiously at Carter. The man puts fear in her and I don't like it at all.

What the fuck does he do to her behind closed doors? I have to make this Carter's decision to sit here; otherwise, she'll be afraid the whole night.

"My understanding was you wanted to play with the big boys, Carter? Do you prefer to sit elsewhere?" I prompt, poking at Carter's ego. I glance over at him. The vein in his neck is bulging. He's biting his tongue hard. "Well?"

"The Boss shouldn't have to ask twice," Giovanni snaps.

"Yeah. Fine. The tramp can sit wherever," Carter mutters.

Red fills my sight and, without thought, I grab the collar of his fucking shirt and yank him inches from my face. A few of my other guys rush across the room and over to the table. I lean close to Carter's ear.

"This is your first and last fucking warning," I whisper. "If you call her outside her name again, you won't live to do it again."

I release his shirt forcefully, and he teeters back. He straightens his suit with his eyes locked on me. I'll be damned if I let a piss ant like him disrespect Eva.

"Understood," Carter finally replies and sits in the other chair.

I turn my attention to Eva. Her expression is hard to read. I can't tell if she's afraid, thankful, or annoyed by my gesture.

"Miss Merrick," I say calmly, smiling. She nods her head, then walks around the chair and sits down. I help move the chair forward. "See to it that Miss Merrick has a personal waitress."

"On it, Boss," Eddie replies before heading off to track down a waitress.

I glare at Carter and then look at Giovanni, who nods knowingly. Not a word is spoken between us as I take my seat once more. Everyone is staring at me. I look up and they quickly go back to pretending to mind their business.

"Let's get this show on the road," I motion for Clarice to go deal the cards.

"You're the boss." She smiles brightly and shuffles the cards. "Alright, fellas, place your bets now."

Four hands have been gone by. Each time, Carter tried to keep up with all of our bets instead of tossing his hand. He's either a bigger dumbass than I thought or a complete egotistical maniac.

Eva has barely moved a muscle. She politely accepted a water from the waitress, at the beginning of the first hand. Since then, she's been as quiet as a mouse. Occasionally, I'll catch her glancing at me; however, it doesn't last long before her eyes are lowered on her lap.

"All in," I call, pushing all my chips into the center of the table.

"This is horseshit!" Carter shouts, tossing his cards down into the middle of the table.

"Carter," Eva whispers, leaning over to him. He cuts his eyes at her.

She quickly straightens her back and looks forward.

My fists ball as I watch her silently put back into *her place.* This guy is a real piece of shit.

"I'm not done. I'll call my father and have him wire me some money," Carter declares.

"Classy," I smirk, rolling my eyes. The others around the table laugh.

"You just know that I'm going to beat your fucking hand," he snaps. Giovanni pushes out of his chair so fast, which causes the enforcers in the room to rush over. I hold up my hand and the room comes to a halt. Eva is biting her bottom lip nervously as she looks back and forth between Carter and Giovanni.

"I just need five minutes to get more money," Carter says, unamused by everything.

"This is a poker game, not an arcade," I reply coolie. "The game just called for all-in. If you don't have the funds, then you're out."

Carter scoffs and runs his hands through his hair. The wheels are turning in his head, but I'm pretty sure the hamster turning them is dead. His eyes finally land on Eva and he gestures at her.

"Her. You can have her!" he shouts for the whole fucking room to hear.

"Are you honestly betting your girl?" I chuckle, leaning back in my seat.

"You want her. You can have her.." he smirks, "... if you win."

CHAPTER FIVE
EVA

My head snaps in Carter's direction when I hear his
words. No, I thought. He was joking. He had to be.
Carter did not just use me as a bet in his poker game. He
wouldn't stoop that low, would he? Marco asks if he was seriously betting me and Carter replied with a yes. It felt like a
punch to my stomach.

I sat stunned as the entire room fell silent, waiting for
Marco's reply. Surely he wouldn't agree to this. This was
insane. No sane person would accept such a thing. I turned to
look at him, my heart racing in my chest. Marco leans back in
his chair, the corner of his mouth curving into a wicked grin
as he stares at Carter. I knew, just by the look in his eyes, what
he would say.

"I'll accept your bet. If I win, you will have no contact with Ms. Merrick ever again. You will not speak to her, you will not look at her. You will forget she ever existed. Am I clear?"

Carter was silent for a moment. I could see in his eyes that he was torn. There was a chance he would lose, a very good chance, and he knew this. He glances around the room before returning his attention back to Marco. Not once did he look at me.

"Agreed." He replies.

I felt like all the air left my lungs. These two men were talking about me as if I were nothing more than an object. I wasn't sure if I should be furious or relieved. Or both.

"Carter, what are you doing?" I ask, unbelieving at how far he will go to prove himself to these people. Carter looks at me, no expression on his face.

"Playing a game." He simply replies. I had no idea what to think, what to do.

If Carter wins, not only would he be happy he had bested a man that holds more power than anyone can imagine, but he would prove to this world he is a force to be reckoned with. But I knew, no matter what, when we return home later on, I would pay dearly for tonight's events. Carter would blame me for all of it. Stating that I flirted or encouraged it. If Marco wins, I would finally be free of Carter's hold, but a thought remains. What were his plans for me if he did win? Would Marco be a bigger monster than Carter?

Marco turns his head to the dealer and motions to her to begin. The cards were shuffled, then dealt out to both men.

The game has begun. I inhale a breath, my heart racing even faster, if that was even possible, as the fate of my life was in the hands of these two men. There were a few whispers throughout the entire room, but then everyone fell silent once again. The tension in the air was so thick you could slice it with a knife. Everyone seemed to hold their breaths as they watch this unfold. Each man lifted their cards.

The dealer waits, Carter, asking for two cards in exchange for two. Marco holding. Then came the time to see who will be the victor. My heart seemed to stop as Marco asks Carter to reveal his hand. Carter turns his eyes to mine with a smile, then lays his cards down on the table for all to see.

"A straight flush," the dealer announces. I had no clue how to play poker, but I'd heard enough from Carter to know that was a very good hand. Carter grins at his opponent, clearly thinking that he had won. The dealer turns to Marco. "Mr. Giodano?"

Marco remains silent, his eyes on Carter, who is clearly gloating. He sighs, then places his cards down on the table, faces up.

"A royal flush," he says smugly.

The smile on Carter's face instantly falls, replacing it with a look of anger.

"Bullshit," he growls as he stands up quickly, knocking his chair over. "You cheated!" He yells. Suddenly, men were surrounding him and I notice a few placing their hands on weapons.

"Carter," I say softly as I rise to my feet, hoping to calm the situation. His eyes turn in my direction.

"This son of a bitch cheated. He had this planned all along," he snarls. "He was probably plotting this since the moment he laid eyes on you." His angry eyes turn back to Marco, who remains seated.

"Do I need to remind you that you were the one who decided to bet your girl?" Marco states calmly.

Carter was fuming.

"You cheated." He motions to the dealer. "This bitch is on your payroll." He looks at me. "We're leaving." He takes a step towards me, his hand reaching out to grab mine, but before he could touch me, one of the men grabbed Carter's arm and bent it behind his back, then slammed Carter's face down onto the table. Carter grunts in pain then struggles to break free.

Marco rises to his feet and motions to the man holding Carter. He lifts Carter up and turns him, so he is facing us, blood pouring from his nose. Marco approaches him, his face inches from Carter's as he speaks.

"No one insults me or any of my guests in my own home." He turns his eyes to the man holding Carter. "Ivan, see to it that he has a seat. I'll be down there shortly."

"Yes, boss." Ivan yanks on Carter, pulling him towards the door.

"NO!" Carter yells. "Eva!" he calls to me, trying his best to shake the men holding him off so he could get to me, but he was unsuccessful. I watch in silence as they drag Carter from the room.

"Clear the room," Marco says to another man as he approaches me. The man nods his head then was off.

When Marco comes to a stop before me, I raise my eyes to his.

"What will you do with him? Carter, I mean?"

The corner of his mouth curls up in a grin, and I feel my heart flutter.

"Are you going to kill him?" I ask, wanting to know what he was planning. This man was dangerous. There was no doubt in my mind about that. Would he kill Carter? I had a feeling that was exactly what was about to happen.

"Do you care what I do with him?" he asks me.

I shrug a shoulder.

"Just curious," I say stoically. I didn't care. Carter had hurt me more times than I could count, but that didn't mean I wanted him dead? Then again... "Did you set this up?" I ask, needing to know.

"No," he replies and I could see my question upsets him. I turn to watch the last of the guest exit the room. All looking in our direction as they leave.

I wrap my arms around my middle, suddenly chilled. "Do you always win women at poker games?"

He looks at me and grins before motioning to one of the servers to bring him a drink. When the woman approaches, he asked if I would like one. I wave him off with a soft reply.

Once it was just the two of us again, I couldn't help but ask. "What do you plan to do with me, now that you've won me? Am I your property now?"

CHAPTER SIX
MARCO

"My property?" I ask, trying to hold back my annoyance. It isn't Eva's fault. I know Carter has done a number on her mentally. Probably even physically, too.

"I just–" she begins, but I shake my head and she stops.

"Miss Merrick–"

"Eva," she corrects sheepishly, making me smile.

"Eva, I don't own anyone," I inform her in a soft tone. "Even my guys are free to walk away at any time."

"Really?" Her eyebrow raised and I can tell she isn't buying what I'm saying. I wonder what all she knows about me.

I'm sure the streets are flooded with rumors about me being a mob boss. I don't deny what or who I am; however, even a guy like me has morals he lives by. I don't own people. People who work for me are here on their own accord. And they can quit at any time.

The only rule is: they keep their fucking mouth shut about what all they've seen or they die. Simple as that.

"Yes. Really," I chuckle. "I don't own people, Eva. I'm not a complete monster."

"So… what happens now?"

"Well, you're free to go, if you'd like," I gesture towards the exit. "Or you are welcome to stay here. You'd be under my protection, and Carter won't go anywhere near you."

"You aren't going to kill him?" she questions, making me laugh.

Eva is one of the few people to ever question me about something so bold. Usually, people tiptoe around that kind of question. Not Eva. She's shy but bold at the same time.

"Maybe I should take you downstairs and let you take a few whacks at him with a metal bat or a crowbar." My words have her eyes wide and she's turned a few shades paler. "I'm kidding, Eva."

I smile to ease her fear, but honestly, I wasn't fucking kidding. A few hits to Carter could do her a world of good. Who knows, she might even kill the fucker with all the emotions she has locked away deep inside her.

"What happens if I leave?" she asks with her eyes lowered, her fingers are fidgeting with the edge of the poker table.

"Eva…" I begin to reach for her face to lift her chin but drop my hand back to my side. She looks at me. "If you choose to leave here, I give you my word that you'll be under my protection."

"For how long?" she whispers.

How long should I protect a woman like Eva Merrick? I wonder to myself.

She's beautiful with the right amount of curves. Graceful and elegant when she enters a room. Knows how to play the survival game better than most. Everything about her is perfect.

"Forever," I grin. Eva sucks in a sharp breath as she blushes brightly. "Do you like the thought of being under my protection forever?"

"I–I just–" she stammers.

"Relax, Eva," I smile. "Are you hungry?"

"What?"

"Food. Would you like some?" I joke.

"Well, I am a little hungry, I guess."

I offer the crook of my arm to her. She looks at it for a while before hesitantly slipping her arm into it. Slowly, I escort her out of the room and towards the dining room. Two of my guys–Carlito and Max–follow close in step. Eva glances back over her shoulder at them, then straight ahead.

"What kind of food are you in the mood for?" I ask.

"Whatever you eat is fine with me."

"Eva," I chuckle, "I don't think you understand. The sky is the limit for you now. If you want it, I'll make it happen."

She tenses but doesn't miss a step as we continue walking.

"Italian? Chinese? Mexican? What kind of food do you like?" I prompt, hoping that she'll relax and open up.

Most women jump on the chance to be spoiled, but not Eva, which doesn't surprise me. She's definitely one of a kind, to say the least.

"Italian is my favorite," she smiles. It's the first smile I've seen since she arrived.

"Italian it is then."

Eva and I talked very little while we waited for the food to be prepared. The talking was even smaller as we ate. I could tell there was a lot on her mind, but I wasn't about to pressure her into talking to me. I figured she would talk when she was ready. Or at least I hoped she would. I still didn't know what her decision was about her leaving or staying here.

Why the fuck had I invited her to live here? I curse to myself.

I loved the bachelor life. Why was I trying to ruin all that by having some woman, who I didn't even know, live with me? That'd ruin my chances of having other women around. Well, I guess I could still have other women, but truth was, after seeing Eva, I didn't want any of them.

What the fuck have I gotten myself into?

"Hey, Boss. Sorry to interrupt," Ivan says, standing in the doorway of the dining room. I look over my shoulder at him. "Sorry, Boss."

"What is it?" I ask, setting my napkin on top of my empty plate.

"Um… Well…" he glances at Eva, then back at me. Whatever it is, he doesn't want to say it in front of her.

I motion for him to approach. He quickly makes his way over to me and leans over to my ear.

"It's about Kazimir," he whispers, making me ball my hands into fists.

Kazimir is a Russian fuck who used to deliver for me. I took him at the word of one of my guys. Over thirty grand of my product upped and walked away one day while he was delivering the truck. The next day, he disappeared. I've spent the past two weeks searching for him with no fucking success.

"What about him?" I growl. Eva glances across the table at me. I give her an apologetic look then look at Ivan.

"The Santoros picked him up and hand delivered him. Nico sends his regards."

"The Santoros?" I chuckle.

With Kazimir's connections to Chicago, I took a chance and reached out to my old friend Nico Santoro. He's an underboss to the Santoro Family. His father controls most of Chicago.

"Even put a bow on his head," Ivan grins.

"That other fucker," I laugh. "Alright, I'll be down in a minute."

"Sounds good, Boss."

Ivan looks at Eva, nods his head, then leaves the room. I look at Eva and smile.

"It seems business calls. Would you mind if I excuse myself for a moment? You are welcomed to freshen up, then wait in the living room and watch some tv. Or you can freshen up and wait in the den. I have an excellent selection of books," I offer.

"I don't want to hold you up from business," she whispers. "I could always leave and–"

"No," I shake my head. "We haven't discussed things yet, Eva. Let me take care of something real quick and then I'll–"

"Can I come down there with you?"

Her words hit me like a ton of bricks. I find myself speechless and dumbfounded. Little Miss Innocent Eva Merrick wants to come witness the fun? Part of me wants to tell her no because she shouldn't be exposed to that lifestyle; however, the other part of me is so fucking turned on, I want to pick her up over my shoulders and carry her downstairs, then fuck her in front of Kazimir and Carter.

"You're playing with fire, Eva," I warn, grinning. She bites her bottom lip, and I watch closely as she takes a deep breath.

"I'll freshen up and wait in the living room," she says softly.

"As you wish." I stand up. "Let me show you where everything is."

A few minutes later, Eva is sitting comfortably on the couch and I'm walking downstairs into the basement. As I pass my men, they quickly get out of my fucking way. They know I'm pissed and ready to bash heads in.

"Close the fucking doors. No interruptions," I growl, walking into the meat locker. The doors close behind me.

Kazimir is in the middle of the room, tied to a chair with a gag in his mouth. There's a giant red bow on his head. If I wasn't so fucking mad, I'd be laughing at Nico's humor.

"Take the gag out," I order, then remove my jacket. I toss it onto a nearby chair, while Giovanni takes the gag out. Slowly, I make my way over to Kazimir while rolling up my sleeves.

"Mr. Giodano, it's not what you think. I swear to–" Kazimir blurts. His words are cut off when my fist connects to his nose. He screams out in pain.

"Boss, here," Ivan walks over to me with two things in his hand. A tire iron and a metal pipe. "Don't mess up your hands on this trash, Boss."

"Thanks," I smirk and grab the metal pipe.

"Mr. Giodano, please, it's not what you think! I swear!" Kazimir screams, blood dripping down his nose.

"Not what I fucking think? Not what I fucking think!" I yell. "So you aren't a piece of fucking shit who stole from me?"

The metal pipe strikes his chest before he has a chance to speak. He screams bloody murder, tears streaming down his face. I hit him two more times. Each time harder than the one before. His screams so loud they could wake the fucking dead.

"Did you forget who the fuck I am?" I ask, walking a full circle around him. "I'm Marco Giodano. And no one steals from me and lives to talk about it."

CHAPTER SEVEN
EVA

I stare at the television, but my mind is not focusing on what was playing. Instead, I sit and wonder what the hell happened. How did everything go astray? Carter was going to play a game. I was going to do everything I could to not be seen, yet somehow it all fell apart. Now I was in the hands of one of the most dangerous men in the city, who at this very moment could be ending Carter's life.

I inhale a deep breath. Why did the very thought of that excite me? Was I so messed up that the thought of being around that kind of danger and violence was a turn on? Or was it the man himself?

I stand and move across the room to the windows. Moving the curtain aside, I peer out. From here, I could see the city lights twinkling in the darkness. It looks like a million jewels. I think of Marco's words.

I could stay here with him, he would protect me. The only one I truly need protecting from is Carter. I knew without a doubt if he survives this night, he will never stop coming for me. I am his property and he will want to get me back. I think about where I will live if I was away from Carter.

Sadly, I have nowhere to go. I have no family. No friends, thanks to Carter.

He made sure that anyone who had ever gotten close to me was chased away. I couldn't speak to anyone of the opposite sex without him blowing up at me, accusing me of wanting to have sex with them. I eventually stopped because it was no longer worth it. I had a few girl friends but Carter would never allow me time to hang out with them to go shopping or just to enjoy coffee and a conversation. Again, I stopped trying because it was no longer worth it to have to deal with him. So I withdrew from everyone around me.

I turn from the window and look around the room. Marco said I could stay if I wanted, but for how long? My thoughts turn to the man himself. Marco Giodano was every woman's fantasy. Rich, powerful, and dangerous. His short dark hair was neatly trimmed, his tanned form well defined with lean hard muscle. He was both handsome and sexy, which made for a deadly combination.

What would Marco expect of me if I did stay? Would he expect me to sleep with him? The very thought had butterflies dancing in my belly, as I imagined what it would be like to have sex with him. My body instantly reacted to the very idea of it.

I startled when the door to the room opened, my heart pounding in my chest as I turn. The woman who had served me during the poker game enters the room. She smiles at me as she approaches.

"Would you be needing anything, Miss? Maybe something to drink? A glass of wine?" She asks as she clasps her hands together in front of her, waiting for my answer.

"No, thank you. I'm good."

"If you change your mind, just let me know." She says before turning and walking back towards the door.

"How long do you think Mr. Giodano will be?" I ask before she leaves the room.

She pauses by the door, turning slightly to face me. "I don't know, miss. It could be awhile. He is taking care of some business matters."

"Thank you."

She nods, then exits the room, leaving me alone once again. My thoughts turn to what I knew was happening. I over heard what one of his men whispered to him and I knew he was also dealing with Carter. Again, I wonder if he would kill Carter.

I start pacing again, unable to sit still. I want to know what was happening. If I were, to be honest, I want to see it. Marco had offered the chance for me to deal with Carter, granted he had claimed he was kidding. The very thought of it, however...It was a temptation that took me to a dark place.

I glance at the door, then slowly make my way over.

I wrap my hand around the knob and open it up, peering out into the hallway. It was empty. I slip out and walk quietly. I had no idea where I was going or what I was doing. The woman who had just left the room I was in rounded the corner. She spots me and gasps.

"Is there something you need, Ms. Merrick?" she asks, as she rushes over to me.

"I want to see Mr. Montgomery."

"I'm afraid I don't know where Mr. Montgomery is, but if you go back, I will find out for you." A man steps out of a room and notices us talking. The woman turns to face him. "Ms. Merrick would like to see Mr. Montgomery." She tells him as he approaches.

He looks at me. "He's indisposed at the moment."

"I want to see him." I hold his gaze as I speak. "Mr. Giodano offered me the chance to speak with Mr. Montgomery and I am taking him up on that offer."

The man silently stares at me for a minute. "I'll have to check with Mr. Giodano."

"Thank you."

He looks at the woman, then back at me before turning and making his way down the hallway. The woman motions to the room I had been in and suggests I wait there. With no other choice, I did as asked and return to the room.

I pace back and forth for what felt like an eternity. Finally, the man returns.

"This way," he says curtly.

I lower my arms and follow him out.

He takes me down into the basement, towards a single door. He pauses, then opens it up, moving aside so that I may enter.

I hold my breath as I walk in, my eyes instantly finding Carter. He sits in a metal chair in the center of the room. I could tell his hands were bound behind his back. He raises his head when he hears me approach. I gasp at what I see. His right eye was bruised and swollen, there was a cut along his cheek as well as his lip. Blood was dripping from his nose. He winces when he tries to smile.

"I knew you'd come. You can't stay away from me." He coughs. Once he stops, he continues, "Were you thinking of me as he fucked you, Eva?"

I feel my entire body go rigid as he speaks.

"You weren't even a thought in my mind!" I snap. "I even moaned his name as he took me. Is that what you want to hear Carter?" The half smile fell from his face.

"I always knew you were a slut," he spat out.

The man that had brought me was suddenly there, his fist connecting with Carter's chin. Carter's head snapped back before he righted himself. I glance at the man who took a spot near the wall, his arms crossed over his chest while he watches the two of us.

I return my attention back to Carter. "How do you like it, Carter? Being beaten, abused?" He raises his eyes to mine. "Did you think of all the times you raised your fist to me as they beat you?" I half heartedly chuckle. "No, you didn't. Did you? You never think of anyone but yourself. "

"You deserved everything you got. You are an ungrateful bitch," he groans. "I gave you everything."

"You gave me a prison." I snap back at him. My hands clench at my sides. "You treated me like your property, to be used as you see fit. I hate you. I wanted to vomit every time you touched me." My voice rose as I spoke. "Those times you couldn't get it up because you were too drunk. I was thankful for them. It meant I wouldn't have to endure you. Yet each time, you would blame me for your lack of..." I took a breath to try to calm myself. "Then you would beat me for it."

"Tell yourself whatever you want, Eva. Whatever makes you sleep at night. We both know you're mine and you always will be." He coughs again, then spits blood onto the floor by my feet. "You'll be back with me, it's only a matter of time."

Never I wanted to scream. I would rather live on the streets than be with Carter ever again. Seeing him like this made me realize the hell I was living, and I felt a weight lift, knowing I was finally free of it. Why I stayed for so long, I realize was out of fear. Never again.

"Marco is going to kill you and when he does, I will be right there, watching it happen." I turn to leave. I had enough of this, enough of him. I did what I needed to do.

I look up and gasp when I spot Marco standing in the doorway, a smile on his face as he looks at me.

CHAPTER EIGHT
MARCO

Eva giving Carter a piece of her mind was one of the sexiest things I had ever heard. It was nice to know that deep inside her was a bad girl. Until now, I thought she was a meek, innocent, country girl, but after hearing her threaten to watch as I killed Carter, has me thinking otherwise.

"Very sexy, Miss Merrick," I smirk, and step into the room.

"Sexy?" Carter rolls his eyes. "You two are sick."

"Sick?" I chuckle. "Sick is treating your beautiful girlfriend like a fucking dog. Sick is trying to control her. Sick is thinking you could disrespect her in front of me without consequences."

I hadn't realized it, but with each word, I had stepped closer to him. Now, I stand inches from him. Eva took a few steps to my left. Her eyes carefully watch me.

"Women should know their place. They're only good for fuck–" Carter's words come to a full halt when my fist pummels into his jaw.

The chair teeters from the force. Both Carter and the chair crash to the floor. I look over my shoulder. Erik and Eddie move around me and pick Carter up. They set him and the chair upright, then take a few steps back.

Carter's cheek is red and already swelling. Not that I give a fuck. If Eva wasn't standing in the room, I would have taken a pipe to his face or cut a finger off. I don't want her passing out or having nightmares.

"You were just a fuck," Carter spats. His eyes locked on Eva.

I reach for a tool on the metal table; however, Eva rushes past me. She grabs something off the table and before any of us can do anything; she stabs an ice pick into Carter's thigh. His screams fill the room.

"A fuck!" Eva yells, pulling the ice pick out and stabbing his other thigh. "A fuck? You worthless piece of shit!"

She takes out the ice pick and stabs him a few more times all over his legs. Eddie and Erik look at me for guidance. Do they stop her or let her continue her rage?

I shake my head and smirk. They chuckle and both place a hand on Carter's shoulders, keeping him from falling over again.

"You psychotic bitch!" Carter manages to shout at her. Part of me wants to step in to stand up for Eva; however, she seems to be doing just fine on her own.

"Mother fucker!" she curses, jabbing the ice pick into his side. Blood spurts out and she tenses. Slowly, I walk up behind her. She looks over her shoulder up at me. "Sorry. I'm so sorr–"

"Breathe, Beautiful," I chuckle, taking her hand and the ice pick in my hand. "When you hit someone in the side, you want to be careful not to hit any vital organs, veins, arteries. That kind of thing. So hit him here."

I move her hand up to a safer spot.

"It hurts like hell, but he won't die anytime soon," I tell her. She looks at where the ice pick is and nods. "Same thing with the other side."

"Oh. Okay," she whispers. I release her hand and step back.

"Sick. Fucks," Carter grimaces.

"I'm showing you mercy by letting Eva deal with you. If it was up to me, I'd hang you up with the meat hook and take my sweet ass time torturing you for a few days."

"Meat hook?" Carter asks. His voice trembles as he looks up at me with fear-filled eyes.

"Yeah, a fucking meat hook," I reply with my eyes narrowed in on him. "So tell Eva thank you."

His look of fear disappears. It is replaced with his huge ego. He scoffs and shakes his head.

"I'm not thanking that bitch for shi–" Eva cuts his words short when she jabs the ice pick into his shoulder. A scream loud enough to wake the dead escapes him.

I look back at Giovanni, who is standing in the doorway.

"You and the guys can head upstairs. I'll wrap up things here," I instruct.

"And what about the other guest, Boss?" Giovanni asks.

I had almost forgotten about Kazimir in the other room. Not that he was going anywhere, anytime soon. Unlike Carter, he was hanging up to think about his actions and if he hadn't passed out from the sight of the blowtorch being turned on, I would still be in that room.

"Leave him hanging. We'll deal with that in a few hours."

"You're the boss," he chuckles, then gestures for Eddie and Erik to follow him.

"Want us to push the chair into the corner? That way, Miss Merrick doesn't have to worry about him falling over, Boss?" Erik asks. I don't say anything, simply nod. He and Eddie drag the chair over to the corner. When they're satisfied the chair won't fall over, they step away.

"Have a good evening, Boss," Eddie and Erik say, bowing their heads slightly at me, then turn to Eva. "Miss Merrick," they acknowledge, then leave the room.

The door clicks quietly closed behind them. Carter has now been left alone with the two people who hate him most. If he's lucky, he may survive the night but I doubt it.

"I'm really sorry," Eva whispers. I look over at her, expecting to see her looking at Carter. She isn't. She is looking at me. "I don't know what got into me."

"Why are you apologizing?" I ask. She looks at Carter, then back at me. She steps closer to me as though she has a secret to tell me. I lean down and she leans closer to me.

"I've never hurt anyone in my entire life," she whispers. "I don't know what got into me."

"Relax," I say softly, rubbing her back. "The basement is a safe place. What happens here stays here. No judgment."

"No judgment?" she asks, looking up at me.

"No judgment," I smile. "Consider this your secret playground."

"Secret playground," she repeats. She tries to hide her smile, but it's hopeless. A huge smile breaks across her face. "I love the sound of that."

"Are you fucking kidding me?" Carter groans. "I'm tied up, bleeding, and you two are flirting. What's next going to fuck her in front of me?"

The thought of fucking Eva in front of Carter makes my dick jerk alive. Her beautiful, round ass bent over the table. Or better yet, her spread eagle so Carter can see her pussy before I ram balls deep inside her.

CHAPTER NINE
EVA

I turn my eyes back to Carter, blood dripping onto the floor from the wounds I inflicted. I was stunned. I never in my life harmed anyone, much less stabbed them with an ice pick. Yet when I look at Carter, all I want to do is tear him limb from limb. I want him to feel just a fraction of the pain he has caused me over the years. He deserves that and so much more.

I watch Carter as he spits out his last words. I understood then just how to hurt him the most. If he saw me with another man in that way, it would cut deeper than any knife or ice pick ever could. I glance over my shoulder at Marco. The very thought of being with him in that way sends a jolt of excitement rushing through my body. Doing it in front of Carter was even more exciting.

Never in my wildest dreams had I thought I would be aroused by something like that. Yet, I was.

I feel Marco's hand on my lower back and imagine it on other parts of my body. I take a step backward, placing my body closer to his until my back was pressed against his front.

"That would bother you, Carter, wouldn't it?" I ask as he looks up at me, a sneer on his face. Even with the threat of pain, he was still the arrogant man he has always been.

"I always knew what a whore you were," Carter says, then spits more blood onto the floor.

Marco wraps his arms around me, holding me close to him as we both look at Carter.

"No. I was faithful to you, even though you didn't deserve it. You just chose to believe otherwise because you wanted a reason to belittle me and hurt me. So you imagined these things in your feeble mind." I pause, remaining silent for a moment. "You didn't deserve me, or anyone else for that matter," I say softly as I hold his gaze. "You're a monster."

"Maybe you should take a closer look at your new boyfriend."

"Marco could kill hundreds of people, and he'll never be as bad as you are. You use people, hurt people because you think you're better than them. Marco, at least, has respect for others."

"Your dumber than I thought if you believe that," Carter laughs.

"No, what was dumb was staying with you for as long as I did." I shake my head as I look away.

"I should thank you, Carter," I turn back to look at him. "If you haven't made that bet, I would have gone home with you and continued to allow you to abuse me."

"Bullshit. You saw another meal ticket and took it. You're nothing more than a gold digging cunt." As the last word left his mouth, Marco was suddenly there, his fist connecting with Carter's jaw, snapping his head back with such force that I thought he may have broken Carter's neck.

Marco grabbed a handful of Carter's hair and forces him to look at him in the eyes.

"Call her that again and I'll rip out your fucking spine and beat you with it." He releases Carter with a shove and takes a step back.

I stare at Carter, wondering what I had seen in him all those years ago. What had changed him into the monster he now was? Or was he always this way and I just never saw it?

Marco returns to my side and I raise my eyes to his as he places his hand on my cheek.

"I want to stay." The words came out in a soft whisper, surprising both of us. I just hope he knew what I meant. Marco had offered me the opportunity to stay with him, and I realize I wanted that. "With you," I add, making Carter laugh...

"See, told you that you were a fucking gold digger," He says before coughing.

I had enough. I pull away from Marco and walk over to Carter. This time it was my fist that connects with his jaw.

Pain explodes in my hand, but I didn't care. It felt good to hit back at Carter.

Carter didn't even flinch, which seemed to anger me ever further. I raise the ice pick I still held and brought it down, plunging it into his shoulder and leaving it there. Carter cries out in pain as I take a step back.

Marco comes up behind me, his arm moving around my waist as he pulls me back against him. We both watch as Carter whimpers. I stare at the man I hate more than anything. Blood was dripping from his many wounds. His clothes were covered in it. His face was bruised and swollen from the many hits it took. It wasn't enough. I want him to hurt more and I knew just how to do that.

I turn to Marco, who places his hands on my hips and pulls me closer.

"I don't want your money. I don't want anything," I say in a rush, hoping he didn't believe me to be a gold digger, as Carter claims.

"You think I'd believe that fucking asshole?" Marco smiles at me.

Relief washes over me instantly. The last thing I wanted was for this man to think that of me. I wasn't a gold digger. I never asked Carter for anything. I worked until Carter made it difficult to do. I supported myself before and will again.

I stare into Marco's eyes, and before I knew what I was doing. Standing on tiptoe, I press my lips to his. Marco groans as his arms wrap around me, pulling me tight against his body.

The soft tender kiss was quickly forgotten, replaced with a more demanding one. He took control, smothering my lips with demanding mastery.

CHAPTER TEN
MARCO

Kissing Eva ignites a fire deep inside me. My dick presses firmly in my pants, reminding me just how badly I want her. She tastes of orange sherbert and wine. Flavors that I'll never forget as long as I live.

"Eva," I moan, grabbing her ass.

"Marco," she whispers between kisses.

"Sick fucks," Carter spats.

Part of me wants to knock him out; however, the beast in me is too consumed with Eva. The fucker can just watch as I show Eva just how she should be taken care of.

"Let me taste you," I say, breaking our kiss and moving my lips to her neck. She holds me tighter.

"Taste me?" she asks softly.

I lean back just enough to look down at her.

Her eyes widen as I slide my hand between us and lift her dress up to her waist.

"Let me taste you." A wicked grin crosses my face. Eva looks up at me with reddened cheeks. "May I taste you, Beautiful? I'll beg if you want me to."

"Oh, my," she gasps quietly.

I trace my fingers up her thighs, up to her soaked panties. She's so fucking wet and I haven't even had my way with her yet. The thought of her juices coating my tongue and dick has me ready to bust. She's my kryptonite and I doubt she even knows it.

"Do you want me to beg, or can I eat this beautiful pussy of yours?" I ask, grinning. She glances over her shoulder at Carter, then looks at me.

"No need to beg. You can have me," she replies vixen-like.

"Fuck," I groan, picking her up and carrying her over to the workbench against the wall. "I'm going to fucking devour you."

"Marco," she whimpers. "Please."

I set her down on the bench. She wraps her legs around my waist.

"No, Ma'am," I smirk, grabbing one of her legs and placing it on my chest. She follows suit and lifts her other leg. Leaning back on her elbows, she smiles up at me.

"Are you seriously going to fucking do this?" Carter yells.

"Keep your mouth shut if you want to survive," I growl, glancing over my shoulder back at him. He opens his mouth but quickly shuts it. "That's what I thought."

I return my attention back to Eva. She shakes her head slightly. Despite how Carter has treated her, she still wants the bastard to live.

"You're the boss," I wink. She giggles softly and then kisses me.

"You're the sweetest," she smiles.

"Ugh. Are you fucking serious?" Carter complains. Eva looks over my shoulder at him.

"Shut the hell up, Carter. Or I'll see to it that you don't leave this room in one piece." Eva glares at him.

Her dark side is just as sexy as her innocent side. Something about her willingness to cross the moral boundary just excites me. Most women run far away at the slightest hint of danger and death. Not Eva. She's danced on the line since entering the basement.

"Marco," she whispers.

"Yes, Beautiful?" I ask.

"Fuck me."

With quick fingers, I work her black lacy thong off and toss it in Carter's direction. He mutters something, but not enough for me to break my focus from Eva's freshly shaved pussy.

"Mmm," I moan, spreading her legs wide.

Leaning down, I run my tongue between her lips up to her clit. Eva's legs drape over my shoulders and she grips my hair, making me grin. I suck and flick her clit vigorously, my silent plea for her to come for me.

"Marco," Eva moans.

Her hips rock slowly, pressing her pussy against my tongue. I slide two fingers slowly inside her pussy. She sucks in a sharp breath and her back arches.

Her pussy is super tight. My cock throbs hard, making my pants almost unbearable to wear. I want to ram my dick deep in her, but if she's this tight with my fingers, I need to stretch her a bit first.

"Come for me," I demand, sliding my fingers in and out of her faster. Sucking greedily on her clit. I want her cum. No. I need it.

"Marco. Marco, I'm–I'm going–" she stammers.

"Now," I growl.

As though it was the magic word, Eva comes unglued. Her legs tighten around my head as her body shakes and pussy drenches my fingers with her juices. I don't stop fingering her, nor do I stop teasing her clit. I want to hear my name echo off these walls.

"Marco!" she screams as another orgasm strikes. Her fingers grip my hair harder, making me wince from the pain. I've never been into pain being inflicted on me; however, with Eva, it's a huge turn-on.

"Please. Please, Marco. Fuck me," she begs.

"With fucking pleasure," I moan, standing up tall.

I quickly undo my pants and work my boxers and pants down. My cock springs free, aching to be balls deep inside Eva.

"Are you seriously goin–" Carter complains.

"Shut up!" Eva and I shout in unison.

We look at each other and grin.

"You're so fucking sexy," I say huskily, grabbing my dick and pressing it into her wetness. "I promise I'll go slow."

Eva shakes her head.

"Take what's yours," she whispers. "Please."

"You never have to beg me, beautiful," I reply, thrusting deep inside her.

Her pussy stretches to fit my size. She screams out, not a scream of pleasure but one of pain. My heart races as I search her face for any signs that she's okay.

"Eva, are–"

Again, she shakes her head.

"Second thoughts, slowly," she giggles. I can't help but chuckle at her words. She's so bold yet so meek at the same time. The perfect combination to me.

I smile and kiss her ankle; carefully sliding in and out of her. With each thrust, I feel her body relax until, eventually; she is moaning from pleasure–music to my ears. Her hands desperately reach around for something to hold on to as I ram harder and faster into her pussy. Her moans turn into screams, echoing off the concrete walls, muffling out any and all things spewing from Carter's mouth.

"Come for me," I demand.

"Marco," Eva moans.

"Give me what's mine. Now," I growl, slamming balls deep inside her.

Her nails dig into my skin through my shirt. Definitely going to leave a mark which is usually a no-go.

I've never allowed a woman to mark me. No matter how good the sex is. I'm no one's fucking property... however, with Eva, I'll gladly make an exception.

CHAPTER ELEVEN
EVA

I cry out with my release as it rolls over me in waves of ecstasy. My eyes drift closed as I rode the tide of my orgasm. Never before had I felt anything this powerful. Never had I come so hard that my entire body shuddered in pleasure. Marco holds on to me as he thrust into me once more, groaning as his own climax took him. His cock pulsed inside me as he collapsed on top of me.

Marco rests his head on my shoulder as I hold him tightly, our breaths coming in rapid pants as we lay together. After a few minutes, Marco rises. He watches me with hooded eyes, then places his hand on the nape of my neck and pulls me in for a passionate kiss.

"Are you alright?" he whispers and I smile at him.

"I'm better than alright."

He smiles as he straightens up, then takes a step back, righting his clothing. My eyes drift past Marco to where Carter is sitting. The venom in his eyes tells me how angry he is, and I am glad for it.

I slip off the bench, pulling my dress down over my hips, my eyes never leaving Carter's. I have to admit, having Carter watch Marco fuck me added to the excitement and pleasure. It heightened it even more. What type of person did that make me, I wonder?

"I always knew you were a whore." He says as he stares at me.

"Believe what you want, Carter. You no longer matter," I reply to him. Realizing then just how little he did matter. I no longer care what Carter thinks, or if I would be punished later. I realized then that Carter could no longer touch me.

"I'll make you pay, bitch," Carter adds with a sneer.

"You can no longer hurt me," I say with a smile. "You're insignificant."

Marco approaches, coming to stand behind me. He pulls me back against his body, his arm wrapping around my middle. Together, we look at Carter.

"What a fucking pair. You two deserve one another," Carter says with a laugh.

"What would you like to do with him?" Marco asks as he places a kiss on my neck. I knew what he wanted to know. Should he kill him and be done with it, or did I want Carter to live? I looked at Carter.

His lip bleeding and swollen, his cheek bruised, his eye nearly shut. I knew he had other injuries, how could he not with the beating he had taken.

"Do with him what you will. I don't care." I turn in Marco's arms and place my hands on his chest. "I don't want to think about him anymore. What I want right now is to sleep." I press my lips to Marco's, then add. "In your arms."

I knew come morning, I would wonder what I was doing. I was freely giving myself to a man I hardly knew, other than he was dangerous. Again I wonder. Was I trading one monster for another? The moment that thought entered my mind, I knew the answer. Marco may be a monster to some, but to me, he was only kind, gentle.

"Let me take you out of here," Marco says, as he turns to the door, his hand on the small of my back as he leads me to it.

"Yeah, take the bitch out of here," Carter calls out. Marco pauses, then turns from me. He walks over to Carter and punches him in his mouth. Carter grunts then begins to struggle when Marco grabs his jaw and forces his mouth open. He shoves something into Carter's mouth and I realize it was my panties that he had tossed aside earlier. Marco gives Carter's head a shove, then takes a step back.

"Maybe now you'll shut the fuck up," he says before turning and walking back to where I stood waiting.

He leans past me and opens the door. The moment he does, I see two of his men standing there, guarding. Their eyes meet mine and I felt my cheeks heat.

Had they heard us in there? We step out of the room and Marco guides me down the hallway. I glance back and see that the two men had gone into the room, probably to watch Carter, or cause him more pain. I wouldn't deny the fact I had hoped it would be pain they caused him.

We climb the stairs to the main part of the house. By now, my mind is reeling. What would happen from here? Where did I stand? Of course, I no longer had Carter, and I was thankful for that, but what would happen to me if Marco decides he no longer wants me?

Marco held my hand tight as he leads me to another set of stairs that would take us to the second floor of his mansion. Again, he leads me down a hallway once we reach the top landing. He pauses at a set of double doors, then opens them up. I enter and look around at the enormous suite before turning to Marco. It only took a moment to realize we were in his bedroom, as I watch him move past me and strip out of his shirt.

Marco turns to me, then slowly approaches. Every part of me jumps to life, and I felt my breath hitch as he pauses in front of me.

"Can I get you anything?"

"No," I say as I look down, realizing I had no clothing other than the dress I was wearing. Marco notices this. He takes my hands in his and brings them to his lips, placing a soft kiss across my knuckles.

"I'll see to it you have all you need in the morning," he says.

"It's three A.M.," I say with a chuckle.

"Later today then," he adds with a grin. For several moments, we stand there staring into each other's eyes. I felt nervous. I just had sex with this man, yet I felt as though this was the first time we've met.

"I'd like to freshen up a bit," I say coyly.

"Of course. The bathroom is right through that door." He motions to the door with a nod of his head. I start to walk to it, but Marco stops me. He moves to the large amour in the room and opens it up, pulling out a shirt, then hands it to me. I smile and thank him before I enter the bathroom.

I close the door, then lean back against it, wondering once again, what was I doing?

CHAPTER TWELVE
MARCO

I t took everything in me to not grab Eva and pull her into my arms. I wanted desperately to assure her that she was safe. She would never go without and never have to fear for her life ever again. However, the look in her eyes told me she needed space.

"Fucking, Carter," I growl under my breath.

"What?" Eva calls out.

"Nothing!" I reply. "I'm going to go take care of something. I'll be right back. Is that okay?"

She doesn't reply right away. My gut twists. She's going to bolt at the first chance she gets, I just know it.

"Look, Eva," I say, walking over to the door. "I'm really sorry for everything. It wasn't my intention to put any kind of pressure on–"

The door flies open. Eva rushes out of the bathroom.

Tears are streaming down her face. I reach for her face to wipe them away, but she throws herself against me and wraps her arms around me.

"Eva?" I whisper. "Why are you crying, Beautiful?"

"You didn't pressure me," she whimpers, shaking her head. I wrap my arms around her waist and kiss the top of her head.

"Oh... I see."

"It's just been a long day," she admits softly.

"I know. I'm sorry for that." I hold her close with one hand and rub her back with the other. "I promise that I'll do everything within my power to make things easier for you."

"Thank you," she nods and looks up at me. "I really do appreciate everything."

Standing on her tippy-toes, she kisses me gently and smiles.

"I'm going to go freshen up real quick. Give me a few minutes?" she smiles.

"Of course," I nod and let go of her. She hesitates as though she has something else to say; however, she doesn't. She smiles and goes back into the bathroom, closing the door quietly behind her.

"What a fucking night," I sigh, rubbing the back of my neck.

Reluctantly, I walk across the room, over to the bedroom door, and open it. Carlito and Max are standing there.

"Boss," they acknowledge me with a nod.

"Go get Angelina. Tell her I'm assigning her to Miss Merrick," I order.

"If anything seems suspicious, I'm to be notified immediately. Anything happens to her and the entire house will be punished."

"Understood, Boss," Max replies.

"I'll go get Angelina, Boss," Carlito says before turning and walking away.

"Tell Ivan to release Carter, but under my close supervision. I want two men on him at all times. If he wipes his nose the wrong way, I want to know about it. Understood?" I growl.

"You got it, Boss. I'll go pass the message," Max nods.

"Alright. Get to it," I turn to head back inside and pause. "I don't want any interruptions unless an absolute emergency. Like a fucking fire, a death, something along those lines."

"You're the boss," Max says, holding back a laugh. "I'll pass that message as well."

"Good," I nod, then walk back inside the room and close the door.

"Everything okay?" Eva asks. I turn and find her sitting on the bed. She's wrapped in a towel and her hair is wet.

"You showered that fast?" I laugh.

"I didn't want to waste water, so I hurried," she admits with her cheeks blushing.

She's even scared to enjoy a shower. I groan to myself.

Carter is going to pay. I may have released him back into the wild, but he will never be free.

As long as there is air inside his pathetic body, his life is mine and he *will* pay for everything he ever did to Eva.

And if he ever thinks of coming anywhere near her, I'll end his life without hesitation.

I walk across the room and scoop Eva up into my arms. She wraps her arms around my neck.

"Marco," she giggles. "What are you doing?"

"You're going to enjoy a shower. Don't worry about wasting anything or money ever again," I say, looking her in the eyes. "What's mine is yours. I mean this, Eva."

She bites her lower lip and attempts to hide her smile as she buries her face in my shirt.

"You will never live in fear again, Eva. I'll protect you. I promise," I swear.

"Don't make promises, Marco," she says, looking up at me. "I appreciate your kind words, but sometimes promises can't be kept."

I stroke a few strands of her hair out of her face. She leans into my touch, making me smile.

"I know that promises can be hard to keep. I won't deny that. However, I'm a man of my word. If I say I'll do something, I'm going to do it," I grin.

"There goes that bad boy charm again," she teases.

"Do you prefer the gentleman side of me or the bad boy side?"

She sucks in a sharp breath and her cheeks turn red. I figured downstairs may have scared her and been the cause of her heavy thoughts, but now I see that I had it wrong. She wasn't conflicted because of the violence. She was conflicted because of how much it turned her on.

"Are you going to be my bad girl, Eva?" I whisper into her ear. She trembles and tightens her hold around my neck.

"I'll be anything you want me to be," she replies, making my dick hard.

"Fuck," I groan. "Let's get you into the tub to relax before I throw away all manners and punish your pretty little ass."

"Promise?" she asks, looking me in the eyes and silently daring me to have my way with her.

"This is definitely a promise I can keep," I smirk, then toss her onto the bed. She giggles as she bounces slightly and finally comes to rest in the middle of the bed.

I remove my shoes and begin stripping myself of all of my clothes. Eva watches me intensely. When I'm finally standing in front of her, completely naked, she grins.

"Guess it's my turn," she says, grabbing the knots in the towel. She slowly undoes it and lets the towel fall open to the bed.

"Fuck," I moan, taking in her beautiful body. "I'm going to worship every inch of your body. I hope you don't mind a sleepless night."

"That better be a promise, Mr. Giodano."

CHAPTER THIRTEEN
EVA

I step out into the warm afternoon, a smile spreads across my face as I take a deep breath. The weather was warm, the sun bright. Marco was off dealing with business, so I decided to take a walk in the garden. I wanted the fresh air and time to think.

So much has happened since the night of the poker game. My life was completely different. I no longer had to walk on eggshells. No longer did I have to watch what I said or how I acted.

I had nothing to fear with Marco. I was protected and safe. I no longer felt like that scared little mouse that scurried away and hid. I wasn't afraid of my own shadow any longer. There was no fear of being beaten if I spoke out or voiced my opinion. Now that Carter was no longer in my life, I was starting to find myself again. All because of Marco.

Marco has shown me a life I never realized I wanted. For the first time in a long time, I felt happy. I knew, though, that I needed to be careful. I feared that I might be falling in love with Marco. That very thought made me smile.

"Eva."

I turned when Angelina called my name. Marco had assigned her to be my assistant if you will. From the first moment, she would call me Ms. Merrick until I eventually insisted she started calling me Eva. At first, she said she couldn't. She would get into trouble for not showing me respect, but I eventually convinced her. But not before Marco let her know he approved.

"Angelina. Is something wrong?" I ask when she approaches me.

"Not at all." She says with a smile. "The dresses Mr. Giodano ordered for you have arrived. They are in your bedroom waiting for your approval."

"Oh. Yes, yes, of course," I say as I start forward. Angelina falls in step beside me as we walk back towards the mansion. "Is Mr. Giodano still in his meeting?" I ask with a glance at her.

"I'm not sure. I can inquire about it if you like?"

"No, that won't be necessary." I had to admit, it was strange to have people wait on me. Not that I thought of Angelina as a servant. I actually considered her a friend. But to know she was there to get me whatever I needed was something I was not accustomed to. When I lived with Carter, it had just been the two of us.

I wasn't sure if it was because he was broke, or because he didn't want anyone to witness some of the things he did to me.

I wondered about Carter. I knew Marco had released him instead of killing him. A part of me wishes he had killed him and I felt ashamed of that. I knew Carter, probably better than anyone. I knew he wouldn't stop until he had me back, or at the very least, saw that I was punished for betraying him. Carter didn't like to lose, and everything that happened had to have been a major blow to his ego. Not to mention, he considered me his.

One thing, besides Carter, that bothers me the most. I had things that I had left behind in the house I shared with him. Personal things I had hidden away. Things that belonged to my family.

I had hidden them because I knew if Carter knew about them, he would have taken them. Even destroy them if he thought it would hurt me. Now I wanted them back. I hadn't thought about them before because I was unsure of where I stood with Marco. But as the weeks passed, I began to realize that Marco was different than anyone I have known.

Angelina and I enter the mansion just as Marco steps out of the study. He smiles at me as he walks closer, then pulls me in for a kiss. After he pulls back, I glance at the men standing near him. They were his guards, and I knew they would defend him with their very lives. I also knew they would do the same for me if he ordered them to. These men were loyal, something I admired greatly.

"Are you finished with your meeting?" I ask, my hand resting on his chest, my fingers feeling the softness of the silk shirt he wore.

"For now." He says as he leans in to kiss me again.

"I was wondering if I could speak to you for a moment." I knew he was a busy man, but I need to talk to him about possibly retrieving my things from Carter.

"Anything for you, Beautiful." He motions to the door of the study and then tells his men to wait there. I enter and turn to look at him as he closes the door behind him. Being alone with him, my heart begins to race. This man is like a drug to me and I discover I could never get enough.

"What would you like to talk about?" He asks as he pulls me closer to his body, his lips brushing along my neck.

"Carter," I say, knowing just the name would instantly cause him to pause. He lifts his head, a brow raises in question.

"Has he contacted you?" His voice grew hard, concerned.

"No, no, nothing like that. It's just... I..." I pause as I try to choose my words. "I have items. Personal items that I had left in his home. Things that belong to my family." I raise my eyes to his. "Things Carter never knew about. I'd like to get them back."

"Carter never knew about these items?" He asks.

"No, I never told him. I feared what he would do with them. That he would use them to get back at me," I say. "It's mostly pictures of my mother and father. I kept them in an old box. But there are some personal trinkets as well."

"Tell me where they are and I will have my men get them for you."

"They wouldn't be able to find them or know which was the right thing to take," I smile. "I hid them very well. I wasn't about to risk Carter discovering them."

"What are you asking, then?" He questions.

"I'm asking you to allow me to go and get them."

"Carter would be there. It's not safe for you."

"You will keep me safe," I say as I place my hand on his chest again.

"It's too dangerous. I will not have you around that bastard again." He places his hand over mine.

"Please, Marco. I wouldn't ask if this wasn't important to me."

CHAPTER FOURTEEN
MARCO

I stare down into Eva's green eyes. She doesn't need to say a word for me to know there are a lot of emotions flooding her right now. I don't want to cause her any pain or frustration; however, her going back to Carter's alone to get her stuff is a big no in my book. There are so many reasons why I want to say no. One her safety. Two, jealousy of Carter even seeing her. And three being the fact I'd lose my fucking mind and burn the entire world down if even a hair on her head was harmed.

"Eva," I whisper. "It really isn't safe."

For you or the world, I think to myself. Carter is a fucking nut job, and I know he's just biding time until he attempts to seek revenge. And when he does come for revenge, it's when I won't hold back. I'll stop at nothing to protect Eva.

"Are you even listening?" Eva giggles.

I look down at her and smile.

"Sorry. Lost in thoughts. What did you say, Beautiful?"

"I was just saying how Carter could wait outside with your men while I retrieved the items. Would that be an okay compromise?" she asks with a slight hesitation in her voice.

"Eva," I sigh.

"Please. These items mean the world to me," her voice shakes.

My heart aches and my gut twists as I see the look in her eyes. She looks so sad. And there it is, the nail in the coffin. I swear I can't stand my ground against her to save my life. She can have anything in this world. No matter what it is, as long as she gives me *that* look.

"Okay. I'll arrange for you to get your stuff," I say in defeat.

"Thank you! Thank you! Thank you!" she squeals, throwing her arms around my neck and hugging me as though her life depends on it.

"You're welcome, Beautiful," I chuckle, wrapping my arms around her waist. I kiss the top of her head. "You know I can't say no to you… not for long anyway."

"I won't take advantage of that, Marco," she says, looking me in the eyes. "I promise."

"I know," I smile.

It's the truth. If there's something I've learned since meeting Eva, it's that she's a genuine person with a big heart. I've never met a nicer person. She'd do anything for anyone and never ask for anything in return.

She's my Achilles heel. I hope and pray that no one ever uses that against me. It's the reason I have so many of my men guarding her. She only sees two to four at a time; however, there are much more she doesn't see. Every camera is on her except when she's in our room or the bathroom. I have special guards following her in the shadows as backup. And finally, snipers on the roof prepared to take the kill shot at anyone or thing that threatens her.

"Lost in thought again?" she giggles.

"You got me," I chuckle.

"What are you thinking about?"

"Just how lucky I am to have you in my life," I smile.

Eva looks like she's ready to drip to the floor like melted butter. I can't help the smug grin that tugs at my lips. I love melting her.

"Do you like hearing how much you mean to me?" I whisper in her ear. She sucks in a sharp breath and grips my shirt.

"Mmhmm," she moans, nodding her head.

"Well, in that case…" I lift her chin lightly with my thumb. When her eyes meet mine, I kiss her gently and smile. "You mean the world to me, Eva Merrick."

"Marco," she whispers, blushing.

"I mean it. I'll do anything for you. All you have to do is ask."

Knock. Knock. Knock.

I growl at the sudden intrusion while Eva laughs.

"At least one of us finds it funny," I sigh.

"Cons to dating the boss," she teases, but then I watch as her face turns pale. "Sorry. I didn't mean to assume that we were together. Or that–" she blurts. I silence her by pressing my lips against hers.

I pull away from her and stroke the side of her face gently.

"Relax, Eva," I say, kissing her forehead. "We never put a label on it, but I definitely consider us together."

"I just didn't want to assume and upset you," she replies faintly. Her cheeks are bright red, and I can't help but smile at her shyness.

"Just keep being yourself, Beautiful. It will all work out."

"I hope so. I really–"

Knock. Knock. Knock.

"Boss, sorry to interrupt," Ivan calls out from the other side of the door. He isn't the type of person to interrupt me unless an absolute emergency.

"Fuck," I mutter. "Give me a minute!"

"You got it, Boss," Ivan replies.

"Business calls," Eva teases, nudging me towards the door.

"Don't you want to be boss for a day?" I smirk.

"No way. That's too much work for me."

"Fine. Guess the queen deserves to play all day," I chuckle and pull her into my arms. "But I hope I get to play later on."

"That I can agree to." There's a vixen-like look in her eyes as she stares up at me. The kind of look that makes my dick jerk to life.

Fuck. If I don't leave this room now, I'm going to bend her over my desk and fuck her senseless.

"Push me out that door or I'm not leaving," I warn her, making her laugh.

"Hurry and finish work so we can play," she whispers seductively and then reaches around me and opens the door.

"I will. I promise." I kiss her swiftly and step out into the hallway where Ivan, Erik, and Giovanni are all standing. "This better be fucking important."

"Miss Merrick," they acknowledge Eva as she steps into the hallway.

"Gentleman," she says softly before walking down the hallway with Angelina, Carlito, and Max in tow.

"What the fuck was so damn important?" I growl, looking at first Ivan and then Erik and finally Giovanni.

"Didn't mean to interrupt, but the books aren't adding up," Giovanni states. My blood instantly boils.

"Didn't we just take care of a rat problem?" I snap. The men in the hallway stand with their backs tall and heads lowered. "How hard is it to find fucking loyal people? Escort everyone handling the books off the property. Now!"

"Boss, I think I figured out who it is?" Dominique, my tech guy, blurts out.

Dominique has been with me for the past ten years. Maybe longer. He has always been able to track down even the smallest of paper trails. I trust him with anything he brings to me; however, I'm realizing just how small my circle is getting. Outside of my time with Eva, I feel on edge. Constantly watching my back because I just don't know who the fuck I can trust anymore.

"Spill it," I demand.

"Trent Carlilone, Boss," he replies. I can hear the remorse in his voice. It isn't because he didn't want to tell me. It's because he knows I'm about to lose my shit and no one is going to be safe near me.

Trent and I grew up together. I consider him family. When Trent was thirteen, his mother decided to skip town with her scumbag boyfriend. Trent didn't have a father around or any family, so I asked my father to let Trent stay with us. My father was hesitant but eventually gave in—and this is how Trent repays our kindness.

"You have proof?" I ask, removing my jacket. Erik quickly takes it from me.

"Yes, Boss," Dominique says, holding up a thumb drive.

"Alright. I see it's going to be one of those fucking days." I unbutton the cuffs on my shirt and start rolling up my sleeves. "Giovanni, I have an important task for you. I want you to go handle things with Eva. She has some items at Carter's. She's allowed to go in but drag his ass out first. Under no circumstance is she allowed in the house with him. Heads will roll if I find out they were together. Understood?"

"Yes, Boss," Giovanni replies.

"Someone go grab Trent and meet me in the fucking basement," I growl.

"Yes, Boss!" all of my men say in unison as I storm past them.

"I better not wait long either!"

CHAPTER FIFTEEN
EVA

I chewed my lip as I stood on the balcony overlooking the gardens, waiting to leave. Marco had agreed to let me reclaim my personal belongings from Carter, but preparations needed to be made before I was allowed to ever step foot near Carter's house. I understood it. Marco was protecting me. Carter was not to be trusted. I agreed with Marco's decision and felt better knowing I would have men there to protect me.

After leaving Marco with his men, I had gone to my bedroom, where I had tried on the dresses Marco had ordered for me. It was a short while after that, that Giovanni, came and told me that we were to leave in a few hours. Now I was waiting.

I turn when the knock on the door came. I step back into the room as Angelina opens the door.

Giovanni steps inside, his eyes finding me as he announces it's time to go. I nod my head and follow him out of the room.

We walk silently down the staircase to the front door and out into the afternoon sun. Two cars are waiting, along with a few of Marco's men, who will be accompanying us to the house. Giovanni opens the door for me and I slip inside the vehicle. Within moments, we were going down the long drive-way. Suddenly I felt nervous. This will be the first time I have seen Carter since the night of the poker game. I knew Carter; I knew he would say spiteful things. I also knew he would not like being told what to do, forced to leave his home while I gather my things.

I glance through the window and see the house coming into view. Suddenly, my heart begins to pound in my chest. I knew I had nothing to fear. Marco's men will protect me with their lives if need be, but years of abuse at Carter's hands had me anxious and fearful. What was I thinking coming back here? Maybe it would have been best to forget these items and move on. As soon as I had those thoughts, I quickly pushed them aside. These were things that could never be replaced. Pictures of my parents.

The car pulled into the driveway and came to a halt in front of the house. Max instructs me to wait in the vehicle while they take care of Carter. I watch as they walk to the front door and rang the bell. I held my breath as I wait for Carter to answer the door, but minute after minute passes and there was no answer. Perhaps Carter was not at home? I wonder.

The door suddenly opens, and a woman appears. She speaks to the men, then looks towards the car where I wait before returning her attention back to the men. She speaks again before stepping back into the house. I held my breath as I wait to see what would happen next.

The door opens again and out steps Carter. He talks for a minute, then looks towards the car. I inhale a sharp breath. I hadn't seen him since the night of the poker game. I watch him as he says something to Marco's men and realize I no longer fear him as I used to. I knew he could no longer touch me or hurt me.

The woman reappears, and she says something to Carter then the two of them walk down the steps, two of Marco's men right behind them. Two more enter the house and again I wait. It felt like an eternity before they reappeared. I just wanted this over, collect my things, and be rid of Carter forever.

Giovanni speaks to the two men, then walks to the car and opens my door. I know it's now alright for me to exit and do what I have come here to do. I climb out, not bothering to look in Carter's direction, yet I can feel his eyes on me. I walk up the steps and enter the house, trying my best to ignore the man that has caused me so much pain in my life. Giovanni and Max follow me inside.

"I'd like to go upstairs alone if that's alright?" I glance over my shoulder at the men before heading to the staircase, not bothering to wait for their answer. "I won't be long," I say as I start up the steps.

They don't follow me, instead, they stay back and allow me to do what I need to do. I wasn't a fool though, I knew the only reason they didn't follow was because they knew the house was safe.

I walk down the hallway to the bedroom I once shared with Carter. I enter and pause, taking a moment to look around. Nothing had changed, except it was no longer my things hanging in the closet. I open the closet door and push aside the clothing, then toss aside the shoes. Once the space is clear, I look at the floorboards. Carter never bothered to look closet at the closet, so he never saw the loose board hidden under the shoes. I reach down and remove the loose floorboard. As I do, I can't help but wonder who the woman is, and whether or not I should warn her about the monster she was involved with.

I pull the small box out of the hole and open it up. Inside are pictures of my parents, who died when I was just a small girl. A necklace that had belonged to my mother and one of her rings. I rise to my feet and exit the closet, leaving the hole open and exiting the room. I no longer cared if Carter knew about my hiding place.

Clutching the box to me, I leave the room and walk back downstairs, finding Max and Giovanni waiting at the bottom. I pause and look around again before I walk to the front door and step outside. The men follow me as I ascend the steps and walk over to the car. I glance at Carter, who stands silently, glaring at me.

I know he wants to say something but holds back. Smart of him. These men wouldn't hesitate to punish him for being disrespectful towards me.

Giovanni is next to me, opening my door, and waits as I slip inside before closing it and moving around the car to the driver's seat. In minutes, we pull away and I glance back to see Carter still standing there watching us as we drive away. I knew it was killing him not to lash out.

"Back to the house?" Giovanni asks once we are back out on the road.

"No, downtown, please. I'd like to do some quick shopping." He looks at me through the mirror before giving me a nod of his head. I can tell he isn't happy about it, but he says nothing.

I lean back in my seat, my finger brushing over the top of the box, relief rushing over me that I had it back in my possession.

We arrive downtown and Giovanni parks the car. I wait for him to walk around and open my door for me after he makes sure the area is safe for me to exit the vehicle. I still can't get used to this. The protection these men give.

I climb from the car and enter the store. Instantly, the salespeople approach me. I smile and explain what I am looking for, and they nearly stumble over themselves to help. I glance at Giovanni and Max, who stands just inside the store, watching everything that is going on around them. I knew this had to be killing them, watching a woman as she shops, but I also knew neither of them would complain one bit.

I walk around the shop, looking over the various items, finding a few things I think Marco may like. A dress catches my eye and I walk over to it, lifting the fabric in my hand. It was beautiful, elegant.

"I think that dress would look amazing on you." A woman says when she suddenly appears. "You should try it on." I glance up at her when she speaks.

"I don't know."

Suddenly, there is the sound of commotion coming from the front of the store. I turn and see Giovanni and Max rushing to the door of the shop.

"You're with Marco Giodano aren't you?" The woman asks.

"What?" I say when I turn to look at her.

"Marco Giodano is one of the most powerful men in the city, which makes you someone important," she says

"How so?" I ask, my attention returning to the front of the store.

"You're his girlfriend, someone he cares about. Anyone that wants to hurt him, will use you."

I step forward. I need to find out what is happening, but the woman stops me.

"I wouldn't do that. You'd just be in their way."

A loud bang sounds near the front, and I start forward.

"There is trouble up there, come with me. I'll take you to the back, where you'll be safe." She says as she places her hand on my arm, stopping me again.

"I shouldn't," I say my attention still to the front of the store.

"Trust me on this, you don't want to be out here when shit goes to hell. Mr. Giodano would want you safe, wouldn't he?" she says, the smile that was there before now gone.

Another loud noise which sounded almost like gunfire echoes in the store. I shake my head as regret fills me. I shouldn't have insisted on shopping, I should have just gone home. The woman gives my arm a gentle pull.

"We should go now." She suggests as she guides me toward the back.

Get safe. Those words play inside my head as I follow the woman to the back of the store.

"Who are you?" I ask as we walk down a short hallway.

"Just an employee of the store," she smiles as she opens the door to one of the rooms. She motions for me to step inside.

I enter and discover a man standing near the back, he turns when he hears us. A smile spreads across his face when he sees me.

"Who are you?" I ask with a step back, but the woman blocks my path.

"I get my money, right?" the woman asks as she closes the door.

"You'll get everything coming to you." The man grins as he stalks towards me. I turn to rush for the door but I didn't get far. I was grabbed from behind and felt a pinch in my neck as I struggle to break free. The room began to get dark, and I felt my body grow sluggish. Before I knew it, everything went dark.

CHAPTER SIXTEEN
MARCO

In one phone call, my entire world shattered. Never had I felt so heartbroken and sick to my stomach. My trembling fingers had gripped the pipe in my hand so tight, I thought it was going to bend from the force. Trent, who was tied to the chair, looked more terrified now than when he was first dragged into the room.

"Boss. Boss," I hear Ivan faintly call out in the distance.

My ears are ringing. My head foggy. How the fuck did this happen?

"We're here, Boss," Ivan's voice booms through my thoughts, instantly breaking me free.

I look and find him standing on the sidewalk, holding my car door open. He looks remorseful. What does he have to feel bad for?

He was with me when shit hit the fan. And, he's lucky too because everyone who was with her is going to have to pay.

"Want me to head somewhere else, Boss?" Eddie asks, standing next to Ivan.

"No," I reply flatly and then take a deep breath before getting out of the car. All eyes are on us, but I guess that's what happens when ten blacked-out S.U.V.s pull up to a mall and men in black suits hop out.

Eddie closes the door, and I head towards the doors. People move out of our way as we make our way inside. The mall goes from loud and obnoxious to almost able to hear a pin drop. Giovanni and Max run over to me. They stop in front of me and lower their heads.

"Not a single fucking word," I growl. "Giovanni, finish dealing with the chief of police. Max, you take me to this fucking store."

They both nod. Giovanni digs out his phone. Max leads the way to the shop where Eva was taken from. There are two policemen outside the shop. Yellow caution tape is tied around random objects, making a perimeter. There is glass shattered all over the floor.

No one was injured during the shootings, which tells me it was all for show.

"Mr. Giodano," one of the cops says, lifting the caution tape so we can enter. I don't acknowledge, just walk under and into the store.

Carlito is standing at the back of the shop next to what appears to be two detectives. Carlito spots me and his eyes instantly lower.

"Boss," he acknowledges. "These are detectives woking the case."

"Your services won't be needed," I say. Carlito instantly lifts his gaze to me. Panic is etched on his face. He seems relieved when he realizes I'm talking to the detectives and not him.

"Mr. Giodano, we know the… special arrangement you have with the chief but—" one of the detectives begins. I hold up my hand, stopping him from continuing.

"She isn't missing. I'll bring her to the station in twenty-four hours or you can come by the house," I state. Neither of them are buying it; however, they know they need to tread lightly since their boss is on my payroll.

"There's a problem though… Sir," the other one whispers.

"Which is?" I ask with my eyebrow raised. He gestures for me to follow him.

We walk out the backdoor, down a short hallway to another door where there are two more policemen and caution tape. They lift the tape and we walk into the room. A woman is laying on the floor with her throat cut open.

"Who the fuck is she?" I snap. The detectives shrug.

"She's on the surveillance tape leading Ev– Miss Merrick into this room," Carlito replies.

I walk over to the woman and bend down, taking a better look at her. She seems vaguely familiar, but that could just be me holding onto hope.

"We are waiting on fingerprints to come back," one of the detectives states. I look around the room and spot pictures on the wall.

"Why wouldn't you just ask her boss?" I reply.

"Boss?"

"She works here." I stand up and point at her employee of the month picture on the wall. The detectives and Carlito glance at the photo and then at the woman.

"I'll be damned," one of the detectives mutters and then fishes his notepad out of his pocket. He scribbles something down. "Eva is a suspect in the murd–"

I slam him against the wall and press my forearm to his throat. I'm seething mad. I now understand the phrase *so mad I could spit nails.* I want to murder this guy. How fucking dare he accuse Eva of killing this woman. Eva couldn't even kill Carter– her abuser– when she had the chance.

"Mr. Giodano, that's not what he meant," the other detective intervenes. "We just want to hear her side of the story."

"Here's the fucking story. Eva left out the back door with my men. End of fucking story," I growl.

"Okay. Okay. Just release him. He's new. He doesn't know the rules yet," the detective blurts. I drop my arm to my side but keep my eyes on the guy against the wall.

"Someone better teach him real fucking fast before I lose my fucking patience!" I shout.

"I— I— I will," the detective stammers. I look back at his partner, who looks like he probably pissed himself.

"Next time, Newbie, you should probably think before you speak. Do you even know a single fucking thing about Eva? Or do you just like jumping to fucking conclusions?" When he doesn't say a word, I chuckle smugly. "That's what I fucking thought."

I take a few steps back away from him and look at Carlito.

"Tell Dominique he has fifteen fucking minutes to make Eva go out that exit door," I point to the camera.

"Understood, Boss," Carlito replies and grabs his phone out of his pocket. He dials a number and holds the phone to his ear. "Eva went out the exit door and met up with us... Fifteen minutes... I'll tell him."

He ends the call, looks at me, and nods.

"Who are you?" the detective I had pinned against the wall asks.

"Marco Giodano," I smirk. "And, I own this fucking city."

CHAPTER SEVENTEEN
EVA

I blink my eyes several times to try and adjust my vision. My head was pounding and my mouth felt as if I had cotton balls shoved in it. When I am able to see again, I look around the room. Where was I? How did I get here? I search my brain for what happened and remember the store. I recall the woman leading me to the back when the gunfire started. There was a man. After that, my mind was blank.

I try to move and realize my arms were bound behind my back. I start to struggle, to try to break free, but it was too tight. The zip tie they used was cutting into my skin.

The door opens and in steps the man from the store. He looks at me, no emotion on his face as he steps to the side. Another man enters the room and I gasp. Carter walks forward, a smirk on his face.

"Eva, nice of you to join me."

The other man closes the door, then stands near it, his arms crossed over his chest. I lift my chin, trying my hardest not to show Carter my fear.

"What are you doing? Untie me, Carter," I demand. Carter chuckles as he approaches.

"I'm afraid I can't do that." He pauses when he is near me. "I told you that you were mine."

"Marco will find me and he will kill you."

"Perhaps," Carter says as he lowers himself down until we are eye to eye. "But by then, it will be too late." He reaches out and roughly grabs my chin, squeezing hard. "You betrayed me, Eva. I can't allow that. You have to pay." He releases my face with a shove and steps back.

"What are you going to do? Hit me?" I say sarcastically. I refuse to be afraid of him. I won't allow myself to be that scared mouse again. If Carter wants to hit me, I'll fight back.

"Me? No." He smirks. "My friend here will be doing the honors." He turns and steps away. "In case your new boyfriend comes around. I can't have blood on my hands."

"Not mine anyway, right, Carter?" I snap. "What about your new girlfriend? Does she know what a monster you are? Or are you still lying to her?"

Carter rushes back to me, and his hand connects with my face. The slap was so hard it snaps my head back. Pain explodes across my cheek and my eyes fill with tears as I slowly turn back to face him.

"I thought you weren't going to touch me?" Surprisingly, my voice is steady when I speak.

Carter says nothing as he walks to the man standing near the door. They whisper for a few minutes before Carter turns to face me again. This time, he remains near the door and the man approaches. I inhale a breath, bracing myself for what is to come.

He stares at me and sneers. He raises his hands and cracks his knuckles, which I am sure is his attempt to put fear in me and, sadly, it works. I'm terrified. I know Carter has every intention of hurting me. I just hope that Marco can find me before Carter kills me. I know Marco is looking. He would never just let me go. I know deep down in my heart he would.

"You claim to care about me, yet you're having your thug hurt me. That's not love, Carter," I say as I look at him.

Carter smiles at me. "I never said I loved you. I said you are mine. I own you."

I had hoped there was some sort of feeling beneath that icy surface, that maybe if Carter truly cares for me in some way, he wouldn't allow this to happen.

"You betrayed me, Eva. When you aligned yourself with the enemy. You and your new boyfriend made me look like a fool in front of everyone." He walks over to me and raises his hand. I flinch, thinking he was going to hit me again, but instead, he caresses my cheek. "Then you had to fuck him in front of me. That was the last straw." He grins. "Now you will be getting all you deserve." He lowers his hand and steps back. With a nod of his head, he motions to the man.

I felt real fear rise and tears fill my eyes, spilling over and running down my cheeks.

"Please," I whisper, but Carter turns away. My eyes turn to the man in front of me just as he raises his fist. It connects with my face and my eyesight begins to darken. I knew I was about to black out and I was grateful for it. I knew if I was unconscious, I wouldn't feel what they do to me.

"Enough!" Carter says, his voice sounds distorted to me. "She's going to black out. I want her awake and alert for what is about to happen to her." I blink, trying my best to not faint, and watch as he approaches again.

"I'm not going to let it be that easy on you." He smirks. "I want you to feel everything we're going to do to you."

"You're…You're a monster," I whisper as I try to stay conscious.

"I'll take that as a compliment." Carter straightens up and starts to turn away.

"Marco will come, and he will kill you," I add.

Carter glances back at me over his shoulder.

"He has to find you first. It won't be as easy as you think. I'm not at any of my usual haunts." He grins as he turns back to face me fully. "I've waited for this day for a while now. I've planned every aspect of it. Your boyfriend won't find you and when he does, there won't be much of you left."

"He'll kill you," I say, my voice low, my eyesight darkening.

"Not if I kill him first," Carter says with pride.

I want to say more. I want to tell him what a bastard he is, then when Marco kills him, I will be there to watch every second. But my attempt to stay alert fades quickly and my entire world goes black.

CHAPTER EIGHTEEN
MARCO

I lean my head back against the headrest of the car and close my eyes. My head is pounding. My blood pressure has been through the roof since learning of Eva being kidnapped. I can't contain the rage that is flowing through my veins. I can't even trust myself to speak to the guys, not directly at least because if there's even a hint of attitude, I'm liable to lash out and kill them without warning.

Taking it out on my men is wrong. They may have been with her, but they aren't to blame. Eva's disappearance is on me. I never should have let her out of my fucking sight. When she said she wanted to get her things, I had a bad feeling. My feelings for wanting to make her happy is what made me say yes to her leaving the house, and now I was paying for it.

"We will find her," Giovanni says beside me.

I don't bother opening my eyes. I simply nod and continue praying for a miracle.

"You should probably eat something, Boss," Ivan chimes in. Just by the sound of his voice, I can tell he's nervous about how I'll respond.

"I will later," I mutter.

"Understood, Boss," he replies defeatedly.

He's right. I need to eat. I haven't eaten for hours. The thought of food makes me queasy. How can I eat when Eva is missing? How can I eat when she could be hurt or...

No. She's alive, I tell myself.

"I want a fucking update, now," I growl, opening my eyes and looking at Giovanni. He nods and calls someone on his phone.

"Update. Now," he snaps at whoever he called. "Yeah, well, I beat you to it so spill it."

Giovanni listens intensely. His eyes widen, and he grips the driver's seat in front of him.

"Wait. Boss is right here," he says, handing me the phone. I take it and hold it up to my ear.

My heart pounding. I'm scared to death for whatever is about to be said. If Giovanni didn't want to tell me the news, it can't be anything good.

"Go," I whisper.

"Hey, Boss," Dominique– my tech guy– replies. "I hacked the cameras around the city. I followed the trail of the van."

"And?" I prompt.

My nerves starting to get the better of me. Ivan may have to pull over so I can fucking throw up. This is all fucking too much. I keep picturing Eva dead.

"Yetti has her," he replies, making my blood run cold. "Wallace Avenue and 10th Street. Apartment E."

Yetti is a ruthless muscle for hire. He stays off the radar for the most part. Doesn't cross into my territory and doesn't harm women or children. I've had no reason to put a bullet into his head... until now.

"Got it." I hand the phone to Giovanni. "Wallace Avenue and 10th Street, apartment E now."

"You got it, Boss. Hold on," Ivan says, busting a U-turn in the intersection.

Cars blare their horns as we whip through traffic in the opposite direction. The cars behind us follow suit. Erik is already on the phone, notifying my guys that were in the cars in front of us. I look out the back window and find them all cutting off traffic to catch back up. They speed past us and take the lead once again.

I pull out my phone and call the chief of police.

"Hey, Mr. Giodano. What can I do for you?" he answers.

"Wallace Avenue and 10th Street needs to be cleaned," I state.

"Understood. I'll take care of it, Mr. Giodano."

"Good." I hang up and make my next call.

"Yes, Boss?" a familiar rough voice replies. It's a voice I haven't heard in months and hoped to go many more months without hearing it.

"Doc, I need you at Wallace Avenue and 10th Street. Immediately."

Doc is the person I call when someone needs medical attention, but we can't go to the hospital. He's performed countless surgeries and saved so many lives, including my own. The man is a godsend when it comes to the medical field. There's no one I trust more to help Eva if she is hurt.

"What's the injury?"

"Unknown," I take a deep breath. "But bring everything you have. Yetti has her."

"Fuck," he mutters. "I'll get the team together, Boss."

"Alright. See you there." I hang up the phone and lay it down between Giovanni and me. I close my eyes again. I feel like I'm about to lose control. Tears are threatening to stream down my face. I feel so fucking lost and helpless, and all I can do is hope like hell we aren't too late.

Ivan slams the car into park and I'm already out the door. There are a few people on the sidewalks, but they quickly scurry off. Probably the best decision they've ever made in their lives and they don't even know it.

My guys rush over and swarm around me. Their guns are already pulled out. They're ready to do what they do best. And I'm ready to let them.

"Hunt these mother fuckers down. No one gets out. And, I want them alive," I order.

"Yes, Boss!" they shout. I point at apartment E.

"Go get it done." I don't need to say anything else. We've been in situations like this a million times.

They break down into small groups, each with their own point man. Using very few words and in less than thirty seconds, they come up with a plan. One group takes off down the sidewalk. Two groups take off into the alley next to the building. And the remaining men run up onto the stoop.

I lean against a nearby tree and watch. Giovanni stands next to me. Erik and Ivan pull security for me, but my safety is the last of my concern. Eva's life is all that matters and if we make it out of this together alive, I'm never letting her go. Ever.

CHAPTER NINETEEN
EVA

I blink my eyes several times to try and get my eyes to focus. Fog still fills my head as I struggle to become alert. My entire body aches, my head is pounding. My cheek hurts as well as my arms which were still tied behind me. My right eye tears up and I discover I can barely open it.

I raise my head and look around. It wasn't a nightmare. I was still locked in that room. A sob rises in my throat and I hold it back. I refuse to cry. I refuse to show Carter that he broke me. Marco will come for me. That was the only thought that keeps me going through this entire ordeal. I just pray he won't be too late.

The door to the room opens and Carter enters. The man that had tortured me right behind him. I knew instantly they were back for more.

"Ah, good, you're awake," Carter says smugly as he approaches me. He raises a hand and reaches out to stroke my cheek. I try to lean away but I had nowhere to go. Carter chuckles. "Glad to see you still have some fight left in you."

"Go to hell." My voice breaks as I snap at him.

He laughs and steps away, moving over to the table that rests against the wall. The table held all their instruments of torture. Carter looks over the various things that rest atop and picks up a knife in his hand before turning back to me. As he approaches, I can still see the blood that coated the blade. My blood.

"I must say, Eva. I am enjoying our time together." He spins the knife in his hand. I know it for what it is. He is trying to frighten me. After what I have already endured, I was.

Carter paces the room, walking back and forth in front of me.

"Before I had to be careful. I couldn't have anyone see the bruises on you. I couldn't have that getting back to dear old Dad, now could I?" He asks as he continues pacing, the knife twirling between his fingertips. "I must admit, it was fun, watching you take each and everything I threw at you. I thought for sure you would leave, or at least die, but you turned out much stronger than I expected." He pauses in front of me. "After a while, I realized I wanted to keep you. You became mine. I owned you." He turns from me again. "Everything was going well until my father disowned me."

He turns and throws the knife. I watch as it flies across the room and embeds into the far wall.

Carter turns his attention back to me. "I found a way to get back into his good graces. I just had to win that stupid fucking game, but you had to go and betray me." He steps back and motions to the other man. The man walks towards me and I know they are about to torture me once again.

The man raises his hand and is about to strike me when a popping sound is heard in the distance.

"What the hell is that?" Cater demands as he storms towards the door. The man who was about to strike me follows behind. Carter pauses.

"Go, find out what the fuck is happening," he snaps.

The man nods his head and quickly exits the room. Carter turns back to me, gives me a disgusted glare, before turning away and pacing. More popping noise sounds, but these seem to be closer.

"Marco is here. He has come for me." I say, the corner of my mouth curls up in a smile but I wince when it pulls at my split lip. "You're going to die, Carter."

He spins and rushes towards me, his hand raises to strike me but he stops before he ever connects. "Ahhh." He growls as he waves his hand at me in a dismissive manner, then storms away.

I watch as he resumes his pacing by the door to the room. I can see that he is nervous, afraid even. He knows as I do that if Marco finds him, he will kill him for laying a hand on me.

It didn't matter if he had someone else doing his dirty work.

I start to laugh, wincing when it hurt my side and stomach. Carter turns and sneers at me.

"If I die, I'll take you fucking with me," Carter snarls.

"Marco will never let that happen."

He storms towards the table he had set up in the room and grabbed a small knife off it before walking to me. "I could do it now before he ever gets down here." He pressed the tip of the blade to my throat, and I felt a slight pinch when he nicked me.

"Do it. We both know you don't have the balls. If you did, you wouldn't have hired a lackey to do your dirty work." I was so tired of him and his abuse. I wanted him gone. I wanted to be back at Marco's home. I wanted to forget that Carter ever existed.

"Don't tempt me, bitch. You have no idea what I am capable of." He snaps, then turns away, throwing the knife at the table. It clangs against it, then drops to the floor. Carter moves back to the door and listens. This time, everything is silent.

Loud footsteps are heard coming towards the door, and Carter moves away. He stops in the center of the room and looks around. He spots the knife he had thrown and rushes over to it, snatching it up. He moves behind me and places it at my throat.

The door bursts open and men file in. I instantly recognize them as some of Marco's men. They have guns and they are pointed directly at us.

"Drop the knife, asshole!" One shouts.

"Shoot me and she dies!" Carter shouts back, the knife pressing into my flesh.

The sound of gunfire stills the room as a shot is taken. Carter growls and the knife is gone from my throat.

"You fucking shot me!" Carter screams. "You shot me in the fucking leg."

"You're lucky that's all it was, asshole." The one that pulled the trigger, Dario, grins before walking over to me. He lowers down and cuts the binding on my legs, then the ones around my wrists.

I carefully rub my wrists, helping the blood flow back into my hands. When I try to rise to my feet, my legs give away and I fall. I'm caught and placed back in the chair.

"Perhaps it's a good idea to stay sitting until the boss arrives," Dario tells him.

I smile and nod my head, knowing he was right.

More footsteps are rushing down the hallway, getting louder as they get closer to the room.

There is a rush of activity, then Marco enters. He looks at me, then his eyes fall to Carter. I knew at that moment I was right about what I had said to Carter earlier. He was going to die.

CHAPTER TWENTY
MARCO

My heart broke and dropped into the pit of my stomach when I came around the corner and saw Eva. She is covered in blood and bruises. Her eyes are swollen. I barely recognize her. My beautiful Eva looks like she has gone through hell and that destroys me.

I stand in the doorway, looking everywhere but at Eva. I'm on the verge of tears and can't give her the strength she needs. I'm going to break down in front of her. That's the last thing she needs right now.

Continuing to look around the room, I find Carter on the ground, crying out in pain. Blood is pooling around him. He lifts his gaze to mine. The painful expression in his eyes instantly disappears. He smugly smirks at me. All the sadness I feel leaves and is replaced with rage. Dark burning rage.

This mother fucker is responsible for hurting my girl and he isn't remorseful at all.

"Take him to the fucking car," I growl, then look at Eva. "Hey, Beautiful. Let's go home."

I approach her and bend down to pick her up. Her arms wrap around my neck. She bursts into hysterical sobs, breaking my heart into a million pieces. I wrap my arms around her. She winces in pain, and I instantly ease up my hold on her.

This mother fucker is going to pay, I curse to myself.

"Let's get you out of here, Beautiful," I say, carefully lifting her up. "Hold on to me."

"Okay," she whimpers, wrapping her arms around my neck and burying her face in my shirt.

"It's okay, Eva. You're safe now," I assure her, walking across the room. I look back over my shoulder at Carter. He's still grinning smugly. He should be fearing for his life, but he has the fucking nerve to grin at me? I come to an abrupt halt.

"Ivan," I say, bringing Ivan's attention to me. "You and the boys can get a few hits in; however, he's *mine* to take care of. Understood?"

"Understood, Boss," Ivan smirks.

"Good."

"You mess with the boss' girl– Miss Merrick– you mess with fucking all of us!" Ivan declares, right before pistol-whipping Carter so hard that Carter stumbles forward and falls flat onto his face. A loud crunch follows as his nose strikes the floor. He screams out in pain.

"Meet me back at the house with this motherfucker and Yetti. Have *The Zoo* on standby." It's the last thing I say before carrying Eva through the house and outside.

My men surround us with their weapons at the ready as I walk down the steps and towards the car. Doc rushes over to us. He's looking Eva over and shaking his head.

"Boss, you guys can ride with us. We have more room so she'll be more comfortable," Doc states calmly. His eyes damn near stare through my soul. He is all business.

Ride with him? Fuck. How bad is Eva? If Doc wants us with him, then she must need serious medical attention. I know she looks pretty beat up, but I was hoping it was nothing ice and sleep couldn't fix.

"I understand," I reply, as relaxed as I can.

The last thing I want to do is freak Eva out any more than she already is. Her body is trembling and her arms have a death grip around my neck. She is scared out of her mind.

"I'm here, Beautiful," I gently kiss the side of her head. Blood coats my lips. My stomach knots as I wipe my lips on my suit.

"Don't leave me," Eva whispers hoarsely.

"Never. Never again," I vow.

Everything I do from here on out will revolve around her. If I have a business meeting, she'll attend. If I have to go out of town, she'll be by my side. Never will I let her out of my sight again. I'll risk everything to keep her safe.

Doc walks out of the room and into the hallway where I'm waiting. He closes the door quietly behind him. I push off the wall and walk over to him. He gives me a slight smile.

"Everything went well, Boss. It'll take some time, but she should make a full recovery," he says, rubbing the back of his neck. "She'll be fine. Just fine."

"Are you saying that for you or me?" I mutter.

"Sorry, Boss," he sighs. "Didn't mean to–"

I wave my hand, and he stops mid-sentence.

"Can I go in there?" I ask, pointing at the closed door.

"I sedated her pretty heavily. I didn't want her in any pain. She's sleeping now. Guliana is watching over her while the others clean up the room. I came out here to brief you," he continues.

Doc never talks this fucking much. His nerves are getting the best of him because Eva is the patient. He knows if she dies, no one will be spared from my wrath.

"Relax, Doc." I place my hand on his shoulder and squeeze gently. "I called you because you're the best. I trust you with her life."

"That means a lot, Boss. I'll always give my all to the Giodano Family."

"I know." I drop my hand to my side. "When can she be moved? I have a guest at home that I need to take care of, but I don't want to be far from her."

"Probably better that she stays here a few days, Boss," he says reluctantly. "But you're more than welcomed to bring your guest to my basement."

Doc's place isn't as big as mine, but it is off the radar, out of the city, and similar setup in the basement. It'll work just fine for what I intend to do to the piece of shit Carter and Yetti. They thought they could lay a finger on my girl and get away with it, and now they're going to learn why I'm nicknamed The Savage.

"I'll have Giovanni bring them over," I say, walking past him and into the room.

My heart stops at the sight of Eva on the bed. She has bandages all over her. She's connected to monitors which are steadily beeping, reminding us that she's still alive. How can such a peaceful sound nearly bring me to my knees?

"She isn't in any pain, Boss. I promise," Doc assures me. I don't trust myself to speak, so I simply nod and make my way over to Eva.

"Boss," Guliani whispers.

"Guliani," I reply, sitting in the chair next to the bed. I carefully take Eva's hand in mine and kiss it. "Give me a minute alone."

"Sure thing, Boss. We'll be out in the hallway if you need us," Doc says, gesturing for everyone to leave, which they do in a hurry.

When the door finally clicks shut, leaving me alone with Eva, the tears I had been holding back finally flow. I clutch her hand in mine and scoot up closer to the bed.

"Eva, I need you to be okay," I whisper between sobs. "Please. I need you, Beautiful. I need you more than life itself. Please…"

My words dwindle to silence. There's so much I want to say to her, but I want to say it to her once she's awake and in my arms. All I can do now is pray. Pray that she recovers quickly and pray that she will still want to be with me after all of this.

"Eva, I swear to you, I will give you everything you want and desire. And, will remain true to you always," I kiss her hand gently. "Please, don't leave me."

CHAPTER TWENTY-ONE
EVA

The sound of a steady beeping echoes in my fogged-filled mind. I attempt to open my eyes, finding that small task difficult. My eyelids feel heavy and weighed down. I blink several times, trying to get my eyes to focus. Once they do, I look around. I am in a bedroom, but one I am not familiar with. To the right of me is one of those hospital machines that monitors a person's heartbeat and blood pressure. Beside that is an IV pole with a bag attached.

I turn my head to the left and find Marco sitting beside me. His hand is holding mine, his head resting on top, and his eyes are closed.

"Marco," I say, my voice coming out in a raspy whisper. I try to swallow, to clear my voice, but my mouth is so dry it feels as if I ate a bag of cotton. "Marco," I say again, a little louder.

144

DANGEROUS AFFAIR

His eyes open, and he looks at me while he lifts his head. A smile spreads across his face. He stands to lean over me, his hand raises to brush the hair back from my face.

"Eva." He says my name softly.

"Thirsty." I croak out, then lick my dry lips. I raise my right hand to point at the glass and notice the IV inserted in my hand.

He nods, then turns from me, lifting a glass with a straw that was resting beside the bed. He turns to me and offers me a sip. I lift my head slightly when the straw touches my lips. I drink greedily as if I will never quench my thirst.

"Slow down. You don't want to make yourself sick," Marco warns.

I take one more swallow, the coolness of the water relieving my throat. Marco places the glass back on the bedside table and then turns back to me. I offer a smile, then wince when I shift my body. I ache all over and I knew it was from the abuse I suffered from Carter's hands. Images of that time fill my head. Carter and another. The pain they caused me. The torture.

"Carter?" I ask Marco. I need to know. Had Marco killed him?

"Alive," he says. "For now."

I remain silent for a minute, unsure of how I feel about that. The pain in my body reminds me of all Carter has done to me over the years. I want him to feel what I felt each time he raised a hand to me. I want him to suffer as I had, but most of all, I want him to see him pay for what he has done.

"I want to be there," I insist. "I need to see it done." I didn't need to tell Marco what I meant, he understood.

"You will." He assures.

I knew it bothered him to keep Carter alive. I know how much he wants to see him pay. Carter had cost Marco in many ways. I can see it in his eyes, but Marco also knows how much I need this. I smile at him and press myself back against the soft pillow.

"Heal first," Marco adds, not hiding the worry or concern from his voice.

"I'm sorry," I quickly say. I was, truly. If I hadn't insisted on going shopping. "I shouldn't have…" the words trail off as my throat tightens.

"Shhhh," Marco says as he raises my hand to his lips. "You have nothing to be sorry for." He tells me.

There is a knock on the door, then it opens up and a man enters. He looked at Marco, who gives him a nod of his head, before approaching. He meets my eyes with a smile.

"It's nice to see you're awake." He says as he looks at the monitor beside the bed. "How are you feeling?" he asks. I can tell right away he is a doctor.

"Sore, my head is foggy," I admit truthfully.

"It's to be expected. I sedated you to give your body a chance to heal." He tells me with a smile. He has a small penlight in his hand and he leans in, flashing it in my eyes. He then looks at my face, checking the bruises that must be there.

"Any nausea?" He asks as he places a stethoscope against my chest.

"No," I say. "My head is pounding, though," I explain.

"With everything you've been through, that's to be expected. I'll get you something that should help with that." He smiles at me, then turns his attention to Marco. "She is doing great, healing nicely, Boss."

"When can she go home?" Marco asks, his gaze returning to mine.

"I say in a day or two." The doctor replies. "I'll go get that medicine for your headache." He tells me. He nods to Marco, then leaves the room, leaving us alone once again.

"Home," I whisper the word as if it has never passed my lips before.

"Our home, Eva," Marco tells me. He holds my hand tightly as he looks into my eyes. "You're never leaving my side again." He states. I smile at him. I have no plans to. I want to be with him, for however long he will have me.

"I like the sound of that," I reply to him. He leans forward and kisses me softly.

Several days have passed, and I am healing nicely, as the doctor says. I'm sitting on the edge of the bed as I wait for Marco to return. He had some business he needed to tend to, but when he returned, he would take me to finally deal with Carter. Yetti, who I now know was the man Carter had hired to torture me, had been dealt with shortly after I was found. I didn't know the details.

All I want to know is that he suffered as he had made me suffer. Marco assures me he had, but not nearly enough.

A part of me wishes I had seen it. The anger I feel toward Yetti nearly suffocates me, but it's nothing like the anger I feel toward Carter. I was glad Marco did what he had to do to Yetti. Marco needed to cause pain for what had happened. He was waiting to inflict it on Carter because of my request, so it was Yetti who took the brunt of his wrath.

I was also surprised to learn that both men were held in the basement, here at the home of my doctor. It made me realize how deep Marco's organization ran and just how loyal his men were to him. I knew they were, but to see it was something else entirely.

The door to the room opens and Marco enters. He smiles at me as he approaches, placing a kiss on my lips. He takes my hands in his and gently pulls me to my feet.

"Are you sure you want to do this?" he asks.

He knows the toll it will take on me to see Carter again, but I knew I needed to, to finally be able to end this. If I don't see this through, I will forever be afraid that at any time Carter will appear and cause me pain once more.

"I'm sure," I say with conviction.

He lifts my hands to his lips and places a kiss along my knuckles before leading me to the door. My heart races in anticipation of what is coming. Finally, I will be free. Free from Carter, free to live my life…With Marco.

CHAPTER TWENTY-TWO
MARCO

Everything about this had bad idea written all over it. I knew Eva wanted to confront Carter one last time for closure; however, she was still healing mentally. For days, she reminded me that she wanted to be there when Carter received his punishment. She even hinted that she would be upset if she wasn't.

I want her happy but fuck. I don't think she realizes the things I intend to do to this motherfucker. The guys and I have already been working him up pretty good. Just enough to cause excruciating pain, but not enough to kill him. Then Doc or someone who works under him comes in and patches Carter up so we can do it all over a few hours later.

I have debated on how far I'll go in front of Eva. She says she can handle anything.

There's no denying she is a tough cookie; however, she's already been through enough shit. I don't want to subject her to anymore.

"Marco," she whispers, capturing my attention. I look down at her and smile. "I'll be fine. Stop worrying."

"Who says I'm worried?" I grin. She rolls her eyes and smiles.

"You have a horrible poker face," she teases.

"I don't know. I think I did just fine in my last game." I lean over and swiftly kiss her lips.

"You're so cocky." She tries to hold back her laughter but fails. I kiss her again.

"You sure you're up for this?" I gesture at the door that leads down to the basement. Giovanni, Ivan, and Erik are standing by the door. I looked at them and nod.

"Boss," they say in unison. "Miss Merrick."

I'm going to change her damn name, I complain to myself. Once the Carter thing is handled, I'm going to work on making Eva and me a permanent thing. I don't care what I have to give up or do in order to be with her. All she has to do is give me the word, and it's done.

"Ready, Beautiful?" I ask, looking down at Eva. She smiles softly and nods.

"I'm ready," she replies. Her words are confident but her eyes and body language tell on her.

And, she said, I have a bad poker face. I laugh to myself. *My beautiful Eva.*

"I will be right by your side, as will the guys," I assure her, lifting her hand up to my lips and kissing it softly.

"We have your back, Miss Merrick," Giovanni states.

"Thank you," Eva smiles at him. "All of you, thank you. I really appreciate everything. Truly."

They all tell her how in some form and fashion how it's their duty and how they will protect her always. Their words seem to help her. Her body relaxes some, and she takes a deep breath.

"I'm ready," she gestures at the door.

The guys look at me, waiting for my approval. I nod slightly and Erik opens the door. Ivan walks down first as enforcer, followed by Giovanni, then Eva and me. Erik closes the door behind us and stays upstairs to pull guard.

We bound down a few steps and with each step, Eva's grip on my hand tightens. I offer her words of encouragement and continue to escort her down the stairs. When we reach the bottom, I turn toward her to ask her if she wants to back out.

"I don't want to walk away," she replies before I can even get the words out. "You're with me, so I'll be just fine. I can do this."

She squeezes my hand, and I squeeze hers back.

"That's my girl." I kiss her swiftly and escort her to the room where Carter is being kept. Eddie is standing outside next to the door.

"Boss. Miss Merrick," he acknowledges when we walk up.

"Go ahead and open it," I say, gesturing at the door.

Eddie glances at Eva and then at me. He seems hesitant.

I know exactly what's going through his mind. It's the same thing going through all of our minds. Can Eva really handle this?

"You got it, Boss," he states, turning the knob and opening the door.

The smell of blood and urine fills the air. Eva covers her nose and mouth with her free hand. Giovanni reaches into his jacket pocket. He pulls out a small container of *Vicks*, opens it, and offers it to her. She looks at it confusingly, which makes the guys chuckle.

"It will cover the stench," I explain, rubbing the tip of my finger across the top of the cream and then putting it just below her nose. "There. Now you don't have to smell it."

"Thank you," Eva smiles and then puts some on her finger. "The smell is pretty strong," she admits, putting more under and on the tip of her nose. Giovanni closes the lid and places the small jar back into his pocket.

"Ready?"

"You guys aren't going to use any?" she asks, looking at each of us.

"We've been in the business for a while, Sweetheart. We know it stinks but we aren't going to lose sleep over it."

"Oh. I see," she nods. "Wait. Then why does Giovanni have it in his pocket?"

Giovanni laughs, and Eddie does his best to contain himself. Leave it to Eva to ask questions right as we're going into a room to torture someone. Only my beautiful Eva would do this.

"Boss asked me to get some for you," Giovanni admits. Eva looks up at me and blushes.

"You really are thoughtful," she smiles.

"Only for you," I reply.

"I'm stalling, huh?" she laughs.

"A little," I grin. "Like I said, you don't have to go through with this. No one will think any less of you."

She looks at me long and hard. Worry is etched all over her beautiful face. She's torn between walking into the room or going back upstairs. It's a double-edged sword, no matter what she chooses. She has to make the choice herself. All I can do is to be there for her.

"I think I should go up–" she begins.

"Not brave enough to fucking face me?" Carter's words cause Eva's whole body to tense.

"Why isn't he fucking gagged?" I growl. Leon and Tim rush out of the room.

"Sorry, Boss. We were changing it out as you requested when the door opened," Tim states with his eyes lowered.

"I requested that to be done a fucking–" Eva squeezes my hand and shakes her head. I quickly stop in my tracks.

She smiles up at me. A silent plea for me to be nicer to the guys and cut them some slack. If she's okay with it, then I will allow it.

"You can leave his gag off," she says, looking at Tim. "I want to hear his screams."

The last of her words are as cold as ice. They bring a grin to all of our faces. I couldn't be more proud of her confidence.

Eva walks toward the door, and I keep in step with her. The guys all move, allowing us access to the room. We walk in and Eva gasps slightly. Barely audible. Not enough for Carter to hear, but enough for me too.

Carter is tied to a chair with his hands bound behind his back. One of his eyes is completely swollen shut and the other one is three-quarters of the way swollen shut. He is covered in both dried blood and fresh blood.

"The whore herself has come to grace me with her presence," Carter spats. I start to walk over to him, but Eva squeezes my hand and shakes her head. I stand beside her.

"Haven't you learned your lesson yet, you piece of shit?" she snaps at Carter. "I must admit, this is an improvement to your face."

"You fucking bitch!" he roars, yanking forcefully at the bindings to free himself. "When I get out of here, I'm going to kill you."

"Ha! You still don't get it, do you?" she smiles. "You aren't walking out of here. The only reason you've been alive this long is because I asked Marco to keep you breathing."

She wraps her arms around my waist and leans against me. I kiss the top of her head.

"He really is the best," she says, adding insult to injury.

"You money hungry bitch! He will get tired of you just like I did," he shouts.

"Not true," I reply, gaining both of their attention. "Real men know a good thing when it is in front of them." I look Carter in his eyes and smirk.

"Bastard," he mutters.

"Don't worry. You won't be around to see anything we have planned for the future. But that's your own fucking fault. Could have just walked away quietly when Eva allowed you to be free the first time."

"Sorry about that," she sighs. "I should have known that this piece of shit would never change."

"It's okay, Beautiful." I run my free hand along her cheek. She smiles up at me.

"You two are fucking disgusting," Carter growls.

This mother fucker has no idea just how *disgusting* I want to be in front of him. I want to show him Eva's beautiful body one last time and show him just how good it feels for me to be balls deep inside of her. Lucky for him, Eva is still healing, so he'll just have to settle for physical torture only.

I lean down to Eva's ear.

"Last chance, Beautiful," I whisper. "You can head back upstairs."

She turns towards me and kisses me softly.

"I'm right where I want to be," she replies seductively and loud enough for Carter to hear. Her words undoubtfully misleading to him.

"Fuck, you're sexy," I grin, grabbing her ass and kissing her one more time before I get to work on the fucker, who will never again lay a finger on her.

I walk over to the table that has an array of tools laid out on it.

The hammer is already covered in blood from me striking Carter's kneecaps earlier in the day. The other tools are still nice and shiny, just waiting to be put to use.

"Eva. Sweetheart. Come pick out a tool," I say, looking over my shoulder at her and smiling. She slowly makes her way over to me.

She glances over the tools for a moment before reaching for an old school meat tenderizer. Her hand is shaking like crazy. When she takes hold of the handle, she nearly drops the tool. I grab her hand gently, helping her hold it.

"Are you sure you're okay?" I whisper, looking down at her.

She's looking down at the ground. Her entire body is trembling. I pull her into my arms and hold her. She immediately bursts into tears.

"I– I'm–" she stammers as the tears pour down her face.

"Shh. It's okay. Just relax," I say softly, patting her back.

"I thought I could." She grips my shirt tightly. "I just want it over with."

"Say no more," I kiss her head and gesture Giovanni over to us.

"Boss?" Giovanni asks.

"Change in plans. Let me borrow Lucille," I say, holding out my hand. He gives me a questioning look but grabs his gun from his inside holster. He hands it to me, placing the handle in the palm of my hand.

"Call *The Zoo*. Tell them pick up in thirty minutes. You're all dismissed." I gesture towards the door.

"Understood, Boss." Giovanni nods and then heads toward the door. He looks at Carter. "You and I aren't done. I'll see you in hell when I get there."

With that, he leaves the room and closes the door. Eva looks up at me.

"What's going on?" she asks softly.

"We're ending this quickly. I won't have you suffering anymore," I reply, taking the gun off safety. "Come over here."

I stand behind her, guiding her closer to Carter. She trembles more with each step. I wrap my arm around her waist with my free hand and kiss the side of her head.

"I'm right here. I'm not going anywhere. I promise," I reassure her. "Just breathe. We're going to end this for good. He'll never hurt you again."

"How touching," Carter chuckles sadistically.

"Ignore him, Eva," I whisper. "Take the gun and hold it."

With shaky hands, she does as I instruct. I place my hands around hers to help stable the gun and offer my strength to her. She takes a deep breath.

"That's my girl." I kiss her cheek. "Now, aim the gun at his head and, when you're ready, pull the trigger."

"Marco, I… I don't know if…"

"I'm right here, Baby."

"She'll never go through with it. She doesn't have the balls," Carter taunts.

"He's right. I don't think I can," Eva says faintly to where only I can hear.

"He's wrong. You're my girl. And you're as tough as they come." I hold her tightly, hoping she can feel just how loved and safe she is. "Besides, you aren't doing this alone. I'm right here with you."

She glances up at me with tear-filled eyes and smiles before facing Carter. She takes several deep breaths. When her body relaxes, she raises the gun and points it at him. His eyes widen. He never thought she would get that far. He underestimated her.

"You will never. NEVER! Hurt me again!" she screams.

"Eva, think about what you're doing," Carter pleads. "You'll be committing murder. You'll never get away with it."

"You're wrong. Marco will protect me."

BANG!

The sound of the gun firing echoes throughout the room. Carter's head falls back and his body slumps. Eva immediately whimpers and let go of the gun. I hold on to it as I pulled her in against my body.

"Three shots," I say.

"What?" she asks softly.

I pull the trigger three times, putting three slugs into Carter's chest. With each shot, she startles, burying her face into my shirt.

"Is it over?" she whispers.

"It's over, Beautiful." I kiss the top of her head and place the gun on safety. "It's all over."

"Why did you do that? Why didn't you torture him? I know that's what you wanted to do." Her voice sounds defeated. Broken.

"Because I love you and care about your well-being more than any revenge, Eva."

It wasn't the way I wanted to confess my love for her, but it needed to be said.

"Thank you for caring about– Wait! What?" she gasps, looking up at me. "You love me?"

"You bet your sweet ass I do," I smile and kiss her lips gently. "Love you more than anything in this world."

"Marco," she blushes. Tears fill her eyes and she wraps both of her arms around me. "I love you too. I love you so much."

"That right there is music to my ears, Beautiful," I smile. "There's only one thing left to do now."

"What's that?"

I scoop her up in my arms. She wraps her arms around my neck and giggles.

"Getting you the hell out of here and making you my wife," I grin, walking towards the door.

"Is that what you consider a proposal, Mr. Giodano?" she teases.

"I'll give you a better one later. I promise. But for now, let's get you out of here and make up for lost time."

"Now, that's music to my ears," Eva says with a smile.

EPILOGUE

EVA

A YEAR LATER.

I pause, looking at myself in the mirror one last time before I turn and leave our bedroom. I make my way down the staircase, smiling at a few of the servants as I pass by. My thoughts are on the past year and how my life has changed.

I was no longer afraid to live my life. I was no longer the tiny mouse that hid in the corner. I was happy, happier than I have been in a very long time. I was loved, and I loved in return.

Marco had made my life full. There was nothing I wanted for, nothing he wouldn't give me. Something he reminded me every single day.

After Carter was killed, Marco had done everything in his power to erase that part of my life from my mind.

He made good on his word and made me his wife in a lavish ceremony. I had told him several times that I didn't need a big wedding. I just wanted to be with him, but Marco was having none of that. He went all out and created an enormous affair that would make any princess proud. It was truly a fairytale.

After the ceremony, he whisked me away to Paris, where we spent a week touring the city, when we weren't in bed, making up for lost time.

When we returned home, I saw a change in Marco. He seemed more at peace. When I asked him about it one night, he told me it was all because of me; that I had given him the one thing he needed. When I asked him what that was, he said, "A reason to wake up every morning."

I approach the door to Marco's office and find Giovanni and Ivan standing just outside the open door. They grin when they see me.

"Is he busy?" I asked when I approach them.

"Just finishing up a phone call, Signora Giodano," Giovanni replies.

I smile at him as I move past them into the office. I still was not used to Marco's men. All of them have vowed to protect me with their very lives. Something they had proven when I was held captive by Carter and what transpired after. I knew they were loyal to Marco, but to see their loyalty extend to me as well was something I never imagined.

Marco was seated behind his desk, the phone to his ear as he looks up to find me waiting just in the doorway. He smiles at me and waves me over. I approach and he reaches for me, pulling me until I was sitting on his lap.

"How are my girls today?" he asks as he places a hand on my extended belly.

"She is kicking up a storm," I reply, placing my hand over his.

Shortly after returning home from Paris, I discovered that I was pregnant. At first, I had feared telling Marco. His life/ our life was dangerous, and I wasn't sure how he would feel about bringing a child into it. If he even wanted children. It wasn't something we ever spoke about.

Days passed, and I knew that I wouldn't be able to hide my condition forever, which meant I needed to tell Marco. My nervousness must have shown because he asked me one night, as we lay beside one another in our bed. I swallow back my fears and told the most powerful and dangerous man in New York City that he was going to be a father.

His reaction to learning that information surprised me, and I quickly realized I feared for nothing. Marco was over the moon, happy. When he learned it was going to be a girl, he was even more so, if that was at all possible.

"Are you ready to go to lunch, or do you still need to do some work?" I ask.

"Just finished up," He tells me before kissing my lips softly.

I slip off his lap and rose to my feet.

Marco stands and takes my hand in his, leading me to the door. As we walk, I think of our life together and how happy I was.

I give Marco's hand a slight tug, causing him to stop and look at me.

"I love you," I say to him with a smile.

"I love you too." He replies as he brings my hand to his lips, placing a soft tender kiss across my knuckles.

It may have started out as a dangerous affair, but it turned out to be the best thing that had ever happened to me.

–THE END–

S. E. ISAAC

S.E. Isaac is a mother of three boys, an Army Veteran, and writes books to help readers escape reality.

Writing has always been an outlet for her, even at the young age of eight, which is when she started writing poetry and short stories. It has always been a dream to have her work published and to have readers connect with her characters. She believes that is every writer's dream--to have their work truly read.

~*Every author needs a starting point. We close our eyes and jump blindly into the world of words in hopes of sharing it with the world. We hope to connect with our readers and take them on a journey through our words- S.E.Isaac*~

https://monsterinthecookiejar.wordpress.com/

J. TRUESDELL

J. Truesdell lives in the wilds of upstate New York, where she professionally fights trash stealing bears in the summertime and battles her way through 10ft snowdrifts in the winter. She spends most of her time taking care of her family which consists of two cats, two dogs, one husband, two kids, and a Hellhound named Bob. Before you ask, yes, she is an animal lover which explains her full house but NO she is not looking to add. The house is too crowded as it is. At least that is what she says until she stumbles across the next stray.

When she is not busy fighting the elements, hungry bears, or taking care of her family, she enjoys falling into the pages of a good book or is in front of her laptop where she hopes to create the next greatest American novel. No, not really, usually she is just trying to write down all those crazy ideas her brain manages to come up with.

Visit her site here-
https://www.jtruesdellauthor.com/

Be sure to sign up to the newsletter for information about book releases, review opportunities, giveaways, and more! No spam ever, I hate it too. If you've read and enjoyed any of J.'s work, please be sure to leave a quick review.
Reviews help authors out so much!

Made in the USA
Las Vegas, NV
05 October 2024

96336592R00098